Sisters

By

Rose O'Meara

Copyright © 2023 Rose O'Meara

All rights reserved. No part of this book may be reproduced or used in any manner without written permission of the copyright owner, except for the use of quotations in a book review.

Typeset by George Wicker
Illustrations and cover design by Sara Marsh

First paperback edition November 2023

ISBN: 978-1-912955-51-0 (paperback)

Published by Horsecroft Press, an imprint of
Write Now! Publications

Original poem (p. 34) by Rosie Irish

For my family and writing friends

Prologue

Lucknow, United Provinces, India, 1899

It had been a successful evening and the guests were gradually departing as their conveyances were brought to the front of Carlisle House. Adelaide had been concerned that the recent outbreak of cholera would deter some of their more important guests from attending, but that was not the case. Robert had been away for a month, visiting the remote stations under his jurisdiction, only returning the morning of their reception. He had told Adelaide that, beside the cholera outbreak, there were worrying signs of another famine. In spite of these troubles Robert had been on good form, regaling the new Indian Civil Service officers with anecdotes about his latest trip.

For tonight, all was light and ease. Adelaide looked across to where Robert was standing, his tall stature and fair hair making him easy to find in a crowded room. He looked very handsome in his evening wear. Adelaide was longing to take off her best green silk and loosen her hair. She hoped Avali had been able to settle Edwin and Agnes as they had been over excited watching all the preparations for the evening. It had been weeks since she and Robert had been able to sleep together, and she didn't want any interruptions from the children. She hoped he had not exhausted his supply of Johnnies.

Adelaide watched as he escorted Judge Rajat Kumar and his wife down the steps to their waiting gharry, the gharry-wallah already making his greeting. When Robert came back into Carlisle House, he looked across at Adelaide and gave her a broad smile.

Followed by a slow wink.

Chapter I

Isle of Wight May 1920

"Mary! Mary! Where are you?"

Her sister's ringing tones carried easily up the two flights of shallow stairs to the broad landing at the top of the house where Mary was lying on a chaise longue with Albert's book on her lap. She stayed silent in the hope that Agnes would go away and she could continue reading.

"Mary! Mary!"

As her sister's voice receded Mary knew that Agnes was walking along to the kitchens to see if she was there. The last time Aunt Sybil had found Mary in the kitchens sitting on the table watching Mrs Parsons baking cakes, she had been most unhappy and had taken Mary aside the next morning.

"One needs to keep one's distance from the staff," Aunt Sybil had said. "It might have been permissible when one was younger to spend time in the kitchens, but you are now a young lady of standing. You need to remember your station and not disturb Mrs Parsons in her work."

Mary had accepted her aunt's admonishment but continued to visit the homely domain of Mrs Parsons whenever she could.

"Mary! Are you up there?"

Mary heard her sister's brisk footsteps on the polished wooden treads and pushed her book out of sight behind a brocade cushion. She wiped away her tears and picked up a copy of Sense and Sensibility from the table beside her.

"Ah, there you are. What are you doing up here? You haven't forgotten, have you, that it's Wednesday and Gerald's parents are visiting this afternoon?"

Mary had forgotten. "No, of course not."

"They stayed in Ryde overnight and Dan is going to collect them from Ventnor station at four o'clock." Agnes checked her watch and then inspected her sister.

"You are going to change, aren't you?"

"Oh, must I?"

"Yes, most certainly. One needs to make a good first impression, it is so important. And do try to do something with your hair. I don't know why you don't have a bob like mine, long hair is so dated these days. Your cheeks and eyes are very red; you're not coming down with something infectious, are you?"

"No, no, it's just that it's warm sitting here when the sun shines. Oh, look, Agnes, there's the Red Funnel paddle steamer!"

Agnes came towards the window and stood by her sister.

"So it is."

"I think it must be the first of the season."

They watched in silence as the steamer crossed the glittering strip of water which was all they could see of the English Channel between the cedar trees on either side of the sweeping lawns. When it was nearly out of sight, Agnes turned to go but when she reached the top of the stairs she hesitated, her hand on the newel post, and looked back at her sister.

"You will remember your hair, won't you? At least make it look presentable and that chiffon dress, the blue one, would be suitable. And don't be late."

As soon as her sister was safely downstairs Mary retrieved her book from behind the cushion and read Dulce et Decorum Est twice more. Albert had lent her his copy of Poems by Wilfred Owen and Dulce et Decorum Est had been a profound shock to her. During the war she had never questioned the idea that it was right and proper to die for one's country. She and Agnes had volunteered with the Red Cross where the grim reality of such things as dead and dying bodies being flung onto horse-drawn carts was never a topic of conversation. Occasionally one of the other volunteers would be absent from their group for a few weeks when a son or husband was killed, but the manner or futility of any death was never mentioned.

Mary marked her page with the peacock bookmark which had belonged to her mother and stood up. It was half past two. There was plenty of time for a quick trip right down to the beach for some fresh air and still be able to meet Gerald's parents at 4.15. She went along to her bedroom and hid the book at the back of her lingerie drawer.

On Sunday she and Albert had arranged to meet whilst everyone else was at Evensong; she would return his book then. The winding Landslip paths were usually deserted on a Sunday afternoon and they could have at least an hour together in private. She felt a frisson of excitement run through her body at the thought of him. Standing in front of her dressing table she inspected herself in the mirror, turning this way and that, tilting up her chin and pulling her long, dark hair forwards over one shoulder. Would they kiss again? Would he hold her so tightly to his chest that she could feel his heart beating? Would he run his hand down her back and nuzzle her neck with his bristly chin? Or he might be reliving his time in the trenches at the end of the war as a stretcher bearer when the remembered smell of gangrene and rotting bodies would start him heaving and retching? When that happened, she would hold him in her arms until he had stopped trembling.

Mary closed the drawer on the book and her thoughts until the next day. She collected her jacket from the back of the door, slipped down the backstairs and out of the house through the tradesmen's entrance.

In the courtyard Dan was cleaning the new Humber saloon, her uncle's pride and joy.

"Escaping again?" he asked.

"I don't know what you mean. I am desperately excited about meeting my sister's future parents-in-law and I need to calm myself down with a little walk first. You've missed a bit."

Dan waved his chamois leather at her.

"You can come and finish it off, if you like."

"No, thank you. And there's another bit there."

This time Dan threw the leather at her. Flying droplets of water caught the early afternoon sun and splashed down onto the cobbles but Mary moved back smartly and the chamois fell at her feet.

"I shall tell my aunt about this most terrible breach of etiquette and she will have you flung into the dungeons."

"Not now, she won't, not with all this work to do. When I've finished the car, I'm to rake the front gravel and then help Mrs Parsons set out the garden furniture in case they decide to have tea on the lawn."

Mary picked up the leather and threw it back to him.

"Oh, I hope tea will be outside, so much nicer than in the stuffy drawing room." She turned away.

"If you are going up or down through the Devil's Chimney watch your step, young lady," he called after her, "it rained last night and it'll be slippery underfoot."

Mary raised her arm in salute and disappeared through the garden door into the lane beyond.

Chapter 2

Once outside the confines of the house and garden Mary paused, leant back against the old wooden door and breathed in deeply, savouring the smell of wet, warm earth and verdant undergrowth.

The Devil's Chimney was where she had first met Albert, not long after Christmas. She had been going down through the narrow chine and he had been coming up. She saw him first because he was reading as he climbed the stone steps, holding a book in one hand and steadying himself against the smooth rock face with the other. She waited for him in one of the small passing places. He came steadily upwards, engrossed in his book, the studs on his hob-nailed boots striking the stone steps with a rhythmic echo. His hair was long, wavy and deep auburn.

When he was nearly level with her, she had coughed slightly to alert him to her presence. He looked up quickly and, to Mary's astonishment, blushed deeply when he saw her. With his long hair, blue eyes, curling sandy eyelashes and open face he looked unlike any man she had ever met. Her uncle's friends were large men of a military bearing with loud voices given to sudden eruptions of raucous laughter and the group of young people her brother Edwin knew seemed to be of the same order but on a slimmer scale. The thought that a grown man might be capable of blushing had never entered her head.

A few days later she had seen him again, walking along the beach at the high tide mark, turning over the big boulders which had slipped from the cliff overnight. She was on an urgent errand to the village for her aunt but stopped to watch him. Just as she was turning to go, he looked up and saw her.

He bent his head in her direction and she gave a half-wave in acknowledgement. After she'd seen him for the third time, hurrying past the front of the house, she went along to the kitchens to talk to Mrs Parsons.

She was putting a tray of scones into the range ready for tea.

"D'you mean that young lad with red hair?"

"It's auburn, not red, but yes."

Mrs Parsons straightened up from the stove and glanced round quickly at Mary.

"Oh no, my girl, don't you go entertaining any ideas about that particular young man. That's Albert de Versey, he's from Durcombe Grange and we all know what your aunt thinks of them up there. Wouldn't open the door to any one of 'em. And don't forget there's that hearing coming up in Newport soon."

"Yes, I know, they've talked about nothing else for weeks."

"A lot of fuss and pother about an old wall, if you ask me. I don't know why your aunt doesn't have it mended and be done with it."

"She says it is a matter of principle. She says that the de Verseys have taken a strip of land that doesn't belong to them and they should rebuild the wall on their property. According to her it's all on the deeds."

"Hmm. Principles are all very well for those folk who can afford 'em."

"I shall be glad when it has all been decided."

"Heaven help us if it doesn't go her way," said Mrs Parsons as she washed her hands at the kitchen sink, "or we'll be in for an uncomfortable time."

"What's he doing at Durcombe?"

"I think he's some sort of relation. Jane says he's there to help Walter, the oldest de Versey boy, with his writing and he's teaching the younger ones. They lead him a merry dance, by all accounts. Now, are you going to wait for a hot buttered scone?"

"No, thank you, Mrs P. I said I'd help Agnes with the refreshments for her embroidery group at the Church Hall and I'd better not be late."

"Don't you forget what I said about that de Versey boy. If your aunt finds you've been talking to him there's no telling what she'd say."

"I'd best not tell her then!"

Knowing that Albert would be going backwards and forwards to the Post Office on errands for Walter, it was easy to find herself sitting on the pond wall one morning when Albert came walking down the village street past the grocers. She studied him carefully as he came towards her. Broad forehead, taller than average and a gentle manner – he raised his tweed cap and skirted around a group of women standing outside the butchers rather than expecting them to move aside for him as her uncle and brother might have done.

When he came nearer and saw her watching him, he blushed as he had done at their first encounter in the Devil's Chimney. She walked towards him and held out her hand.

"Hello. I think we are neighbours. My name is Mary."

"Oh, well, er, yes, hello. I'm, er, Albert, Albert de Versey. Pleased to meet you."

He tried to change all the documents and packages he was carrying from under his right arm to the left so he could shake her hand, but became flustered and dropped most of them. His blush deepened.

"It's alright, let me help you."

They bent down together, gathering up the scattered letters from the muddy road and then stood up at the same time so that they were face to face. Mary smiled. Albert's eyes widened in surprise and then he, too, smiled.

"Do you need a hand in the Post Office?"

"No, no thank you, I think I'll manage. Did you, er...did

you say we were neighbours?"

"Yes, I live at Boniface House."

"Then, yes, we are definitely neighbours, I'm at Durcombe Grange. Well, I'd, er...I'd er...best be on my way. Thank you again." He hesitated for a moment, inclined his head towards her, and then turned away.

"Wait a minute!" she called after him. "The rest of your letters!" She held them out to him but didn't quite relinquish them. "Why don't I wait for you? We could walk back together."

"If you're, er, sure, that would be most, er...yes, most enjoyable. I'll be as quick as I can."

She released the letters into his hand and watched as he disappeared into the gloomy interior of the Post Office where Miss Pryce sat like a malevolent spider behind the counter with her smelly spaniel, Floss, at her feet.

Mary sat down beside the pond to wait for him.

Their first walk together back up through the village lasted no more than fifteen minutes. They walked side by side and barely spoke but it was long enough for Mary to decide that Albert was someone she would like to know better. When they reached the driveway of Durcombe Grange they stopped and looked at each other.

"Shall we walk along the beach to Shanklin one afternoon?" Mary asked. "I could show you the best place to find dinosaur bones and teeth. I have quite a collection."

"Oh, yes, that would be...er...I would find that...er...most interesting, yes, most interesting. I, too, have a...um...a small collection of fossils. I have heard that...er...dinosaur bones are much more plentiful along this coast than in Hampshire. Oh, not that I am in any way...er...no, not in any way at all...erm... not suggesting that...er...that your fossils were at all easy to find. I am sure you must have a very fine collection."

"It's alright, I understand. Are you free in the afternoons?"

"Er...yes, yes, unless my...er...my aunt and uncle are in

London. They sometimes leave the younger children with me."

"Will they be going away this week?"

"Er...no, I don't believe so."

"Right, shall we say the day after tomorrow? At three o'clock? The tide will be out then. Maybe it would be best to meet at the bottom of the Devil's Chimney rather than here."

"I will look forward to it."

As they reached out to shake hands again, Albert blushed. Mary smiled at him before she turned away.

Chapter 3

It was quicker to go down to the beach via the Devil's Chimney but this involved walking past the front of the house and Mary didn't want to be seen by her aunt or sister, so she turned right onto the twisting lane which led eventually down to the sea. She walked quickly, swinging her arms, giving a little hop and skip every now and then when the lane levelled out, sometimes stopping to investigate one of the year's first green-winged orchids or to watch a charm of goldfinches darting along the hedge beside her. She passed the old Norman church, on through the spinney of sycamore trees, then left the path and scrambled down a patch of rough, muddy ground onto the foreshore.

She knew Albert wouldn't be there poking around among the seaweed with a stick looking for interesting pieces of driftwood or sitting on a rock reading, because his aunt had sent him to Newport to collect his cousin's proofs from the publisher.

"Why can't Walter collect his own proofs?" she had asked. "Why do you have to go?"

"He's gone up to London and my aunt wants to have them ready for him when he returns."

"What does he do up in London?" she asked. "He's always going there. And he could have collected his own proofs on the way back."

"No, he couldn't because that would mean he'd have to change trains in Newport and he won't do that. That's what I'm here for. You know what it's like."

She did know what it was like. To be beholden. To be on sufferance. To be everlastingly grateful.

Their similar circumstances were one of the things which

had first drawn Mary and Albert together – they both knew all about being beholden.

Mary clambered over the rocks at the back of the beach, crossed the band of big pebbles and then stepped onto the firm rippled sand. She paused, slipped off her sandals, and ran towards the gentle wavelets of the slack tide. She loved the sea at any time of the tide or weather but her favourite occasions were winter storms. She delighted in the great waves whooshing and thumping up against the sea wall, sending icy plumes of water high into the air and drenching anyone who was foolish enough to stand nearby. The unpredictable ferocity of the sea and wind were far removed from the ordered life of Boniface House where it was always Bridge parties on Tuesday evenings, fish on Fridays, church twice on Sundays and tea every afternoon at 4.15. To her aunt's annoyance Mary quite often missed tea, preferring long treks up across the Downs to Wroxall, along the beach to Ventnor or Shanklin, possibly even as far as Sandown if the tide was right. She told neither her aunt nor her sister that Albert often accompanied her.

She checked her watch. Still time to walk along the sand for a while and then up into the Landslip and return via the village. The sun was shining which meant that tea would be on the lawn and might even be a little late whilst everyone fussed around over chairs and who should sit where. She wasn't looking forward to meeting Gerald's parents but she would do her best to be sociable for Agnes's sake.

She buckled her sandals together for ease of carrying and started walking.

Chapter 4

The dawn chorus woke Mary the next morning. Her bedroom was at the back of the house facing north east - sheltered from the onshore winds but icy cold in the winter. There were fires downstairs in the reception rooms and radiators on the first floor but the old servants' rooms at the top of the house where she, Agnes and Edwin had passed their childhood, were unheated. She went to the window, drew back the heavy curtains to let the early morning sunlight flood the room. There was no sound from the rest of the house. She checked her watch. Six o'clock. If she was lucky she could have an hour to herself before the rest of the household stirred. She dressed quickly, collected her easel, paper and paints and went down to the kitchens.

Mrs Parsons was already sitting at the kitchen table with her first cup of tea of the day.

"Hello, Mrs P."

"Where are you off to so early?"

"I'm going to try to do some painting before everyone else is up."

"Keeps you busy, doesn't she, your aunt."

"Yes, she does."

"Do you want some tea?"

"Oh, yes please. Is there any of yesterday's cake left?"

Mrs Parsons stood up, poured out a cup of tea for Mary, refilled her own and went out to the pantry. She came back with a cake tin.

"Not much, I'm afraid. That man yesterday, he had a large appetite."

"Mm, yes, I saw. He said it was very flavoursome."

"Yes, there's not many people as can resist a well-made

seed cake." She cut the remaining cake in half, reached backwards for two plates from the dresser and slid one plate with a slice of cake on it over to Mary. "I'll keep this piece for Dan."

"He looked smart yesterday, didn't he, in his new uniform."

"Yes, he did, but if there was money to be spent I'd rather have had one of those new mixer things; my arthritis is getting that bad."

"I'll buy you one, when I'm rich and famous, Mrs P."

"I want one of them new cookers as well. Those all-electric ones, save all this blessed coal dust everywhere." She reached forward and ran her hand along the brass rail at the front of the range and then inspected her fingers. "Filthy things, these ranges. Nice electric one, that's what I want."

Mary laughed. "I'll see what I can do."

They sat in silence for a while until one of the bells over the top of the door started to jangle.

"Oh, dear, that's her Ladyship," said Mrs Parsons, turning around to check. "Seems like she's awake early as well and Jane not yet here. I suppose I'd better go. I don't think it's going to be an easy day, I've still got all the best china from yesterday to put away." She pushed herself to her feet with a sigh. "You'd better slip out quick. Go on, off you go."

Mary swallowed the last of her tea, picked up her painting things, kissed the top of Mrs Parsons' head and disappeared out into the garden.

There was a heavy dew on the grass and, in spite of the sun, the air was cold. By the time she reached the summerhouse to collect a garden chair her shoes were wet. She started shivering but she set up her chair and easel because she didn't want to waste precious time returning to the house for warmer clothes and more suitable footwear.

She had been painting for some time when she heard the French windows closing and turned around to see her sister coming towards her across the lawn.

"Why were you not at breakfast?" asked Agnes. "I wanted to talk to you."

"Oh, I had mine early. I wanted to catch the morning light on the trunk of that cedar tree. It's such a beautiful deep colour and it fades in full sunlight. What do you think?" Mary put down her brush and leant back so that her sister could see over her shoulder.

"Mm, yes. Is it really that colour?"

"Yes it is, if you look carefully. Why did you want to talk to me?"

"I wanted to show you this." Agnes held out her hand.

"Oh, Aggie! It's beautiful! Did he ask you last night?"

"Yes," said Agnes, "after his parents had left. It's exquisite, isn't it? It was his grandmother's. He had to have it made bigger for me but I don't think you'd notice. I shouldn't really be wearing it yet because the announcement won't be in the Times until next week, but I thought you'd like to see it." She twisted her hand back and forth and the sisters were quiet for a moment as they watched the diamonds sparkle in the sunshine.

"When will the wedding be?"

"We have decided on October. Gerald feels that there is no need to wait any longer."

"Will you have time to get everything ready?"

"Yes, it will be a quiet wedding here at St Boniface, rather than at St Catherine's in Ventnor."

"Where are you going to live?"

"On the mainland, near Southampton. Gerald's parents have a house available there."

"Does Edwin know?"

"No, not yet. I'll telephone him this evening. Gerald has heard that he's been seen with a young woman, the sister of one of his friends, but I don't suppose he'll be able to marry for a while; he's still waiting for Aunt Sybil to pay for his articles."

"Oh, Aggie! Do you love him? Really love him?" Mary twisted around on her chair and caught hold of her sister's hand. "Love him enough to make you all fizzy inside? And long to be with him?"

"Fizzy inside? What are you talking about? I like him well enough. He's a good man and I'm thankful to have got him. No thanks to you! You nearly spoiled everything." She pulled her hand away.

"I wasn't that late."

"That wasn't what I was talking about. Wilfred Owen's war poetry was not a suitable topic of conversation for afternoon tea; Gerald and his father were both in the thick of things. I don't know what else you might have said if Aunt Sybil hadn't changed the subject. It was very awkward. And because you were late Gerald's father had to stand up in the middle of tea to shake your hand. And you had blue slipper mud on your ankles."

"But I did change my dress and tea was outside so it didn't matter too much about a bit of mud."

"That is not the point, Mary, it is first impressions which count and I really needed Gerald's parents to approve of me and my family. When you started talking about that wretched poem I thought his father was going to get up and leave. Neither of us has any hope of our own home except by marriage, Mary, and I for one don't intend to stay here. We can't afford to be fussy, you and I – Aunt Sybil won't be an easy woman to live with as she gets older. You need to start thinking about your own future, Mary, see if you can find yourself a nice, suitable man. Heaven knows it'll be difficult – these days they are hard to find." She laid her hand momentarily on Mary's shoulder. "And forget all this nonsense about feeling fizzy inside."

Mary watched as her sister walked across the lawn to the house, her left hand held in front of her, fingers dancing. It was a beautiful ring and Agnes would have her own house and a husband and no Aunt Sybil, but Mary didn't think Agnes loved

Gerald, not as she loved Albert. She had watched her sister become a surprisingly different person when Gerald was with her, softer and slightly flirtatious, which made Mary uneasy as she knew her sister was neither of those things. To enter into a marriage in exchange for a house and a ring wasn't something that Mary felt she would ever be able to undertake. She was quite certain that Uncle Reginald and Aunt Sybil didn't love each other. She wondered if Edwin loved his girl and would marry for love, as she hoped to do. Mary knew that Albert de Versey would never be considered a suitable man. He was not wealthy, he had been a conscientious objector during the war and, most damning of all, he was a de Versey and Aunt Sybil was at war with his family. Before she knew Albert, Mary had enjoyed bringing up the de Versey name in general conversation just to watch her aunt's demeanour stiffen and the red flush spread inexorably up her neck.

Unsettled by the conversation with her sister, Mary packed away her painting equipment and returned to the house.

At dinner that evening, Agnes and Aunt Sybil spoke of nothing except Gerald, his parents and the forthcoming marriage. When the dessert plates had been cleared away and there was a pause in the conversation, Uncle Reginald asked Mary if she was happy for her sister.

"Oh, yes, of course I am. Very happy."

"You have been very quiet throughout dinner. It will be strange here without her, will it not?"

"Yes, very strange."

"You are not going to leave us for the foreseeable future, are you? You haven't some suitable young man hidden away?"

Mary put down the orange she was peeling and looked up quickly at her uncle. He was smiling encouragingly at her.

"No," she said, "There is no-one."

Chapter 5

"Not one of the de Verseys was at church this morning," Sybil said to her husband as they were resting upstairs on their separate beds after Sunday luncheon. "That's the third week running. I feel that Reverend Titmuss cannot be taking his duties seriously enough. I shall have a word with the Dean next time I see him."

"Maybe they are up in London."

"No, they are not. I heard several cars going past quite late last night. It was after ten o'clock. And there was singing. I told you so at breakfast this morning."

The de Verseys lived at Durcombe Grange, a Palladian-style mansion which had been modelled on Queen Victoria's Osborne House at East Cowes. Its grand Italianate terraces overlooked Boniface House. Although a lack of money did not seem to be a problem as they had an even larger house in London and another one in Westmoreland, the Grange was badly maintained and the disputed boundary wall was crumbling. Sybil felt this to be a slight to the neighbourhood and to her in particular.

She considered the de Versey's many children to be extremely badly behaved and she frowned upon their parents' relaxed and unconventional life-style. When Leonard had gone up to London to work for the Ministry of Labour, Sybil had advised her son most strongly to have no connection whatsoever with the de Verseys, even though they had offered him accommodation close to Whitehall. Leonard had not listened to her words of warning. When he and Walter de Versey had found themselves in trouble with the law for indiscreet sexual behaviour, Sybil knew immediately who was to blame. She despatched Reginald up to London with explicit instructions to pay whatever sum of money was necessary to have the charges dropped and bring Leonard back to the island where she could keep an eye on him. Leonard had refused to return. Sybil's dislike of the de Versey family deepened to detestation.

As the only daughter of a previous Lord Adjutant of the Cinque Ports, Sybil was used to a more affluent life-style than that afforded by Reginald and Boniface House. Reginald came from a good Hampshire family which could trace its ancestry back through the generations, but when his father died it was found that the family estate had been so badly managed that the house and all the land had been sold to pay death duties. Sybil and Reginald found themselves in straitened circumstances which had necessitated a move from their first home in a prestigious neighbourhood of Bembridge where their only child, Leonard, was born, to a smaller house on the south of the Island. Sybil considered Boniface House to be rather cramped.

"I don't know how I manage," she would say to anyone who would listen, "with so few servants. At home with my parents we had eight indoor staff and I believe there were six outdoor. Poor, dear Reginald doesn't understand at all how much I have to do here."

A further drain on Sybil's meagre stock of goodwill had been caused by the sudden arrival of Edwin, Agnes and Mary after the death of their parents. Reginald, usually averse to causing his wife the slightest degree of inconvenience, had been insistent that his sister's children should come and live with them.

"Of course they must come here – where else should they go? We have the whole of the second floor which will accommodate them easily. We can ask Leonard's old nanny to look after the baby and employ a governess for Agnes and Edwin. I can't see Leonard marrying and producing any grandchildren, so the two little girls will be company for you as they get older. Maybe the boy will take up Law – he seems a bright enough lad."

"Adelaide should never have let herself fall for a third child; she was warned it would be injurious to her health. Robert should have left her alone. Three children, indeed."

Edwin, Agnes and Mary had not had a happy childhood. As their uncle's finances became more and more difficult the money for their education and upkeep was provided by a very grudging Aunt Sybil. Edwin had been sent to boarding school and university on the mainland; Agnes and Mary attended the girl's grammar school in Sandown but only until they had passed their matriculation examination. It was expected that they would both marry as soon as possible and any further education and drain on expense was deemed unnecessary. Agnes didn't seem to mind, but Mary had been hoping to go to Brighton Art College.

"No, sorry old thing, far too Bohemian," said her uncle Reginald when she went to speak to him in his study. "Your aunt wouldn't approve of Art College at all. Never mind all those life-drawing classes and what-nots. Not suitable at all for a young lady, no, not at all. You know what your aunt is like."

"But it wouldn't be nearly as expensive as Edwin's university, so why couldn't you pay for me and just tell Aunt Sybil that I'm going?"

"Wish I could, wish I could. Your mother was good at painting, you know. When she first went to India she sent me back lots of little water colours. Flowers, fruit, that sort of thing. I'll fetch them out for you when I've got a moment."

Nobody usually spoke about Mary's mother and there was an awkward silence between them until a log shifted in the grate sending a spray of sparks out onto the turkey carpet. Reginald stood up, went over to the fireplace and stamped them out.

"It's that damned sweet chestnut. I've told Dan not to bring in any more. Where were we...ah, yes, yes, those watercolours; I'll look them out for you. Was there anything else?"

Edwin, when he was younger, could sometimes be persuaded to recount some remembered detail of the family's life in India. On a dark winter's night up on the second floor of Boniface House with the wind gusting straight in off the Channel and rattling the window stays, he would tell Mary about the wonderful warmth and light of India, the parties given by their parents, the exotic food and about their ayah, Avali.

Avali had cared for both him and Agnes until the worsening political situation and their mother's ill health sent the family back to England to await the birth of her third child. When Adelaide died shortly after Mary was born, their father had intended to return to his post in the Indian Civil Service and send for his children once he was settled, but he had died of enteric fever three days out from Aden. He was buried at sea. Mary's mother was buried at St Catherine's in Ventnor.

Agnes wouldn't share any of her memories of their mother with Mary. In her bedroom she kept a photograph of their parents in a silver frame on her bedside cabinet but would put it face down if Mary ever came into the room. When she knew she wouldn't be disturbed, Mary would sneak in to look at it. It was a studio portrait and must have been taken in the United Provinces shortly before they left for England. Their father was standing beside his seated wife, one hand on her shoulder and an arm around his son. Both Edwin and Agnes were very blonde, like their father, but their mother's hair was dark, arranged in loops and coils on top of her head except for one long wavy tress which had been pulled forward over her shoulder. Agnes was leaning against her mother's knee and she had her mother's hair wrapped tightly around her fingers.

Chapter 6

By the time Sunday arrived, Mary could think of nothing except Albert. She was longing to feel his arms around her and her lips on his. Walking with him across the Downs or along the beach they never felt able to kiss or even hold hands in case they were recognised. Sometimes they returned to Lower Bonchurch through the Devil's Chimney where they could stand together enclosed by the echoing stone walls and laugh and talk for a while. If the treads were dry they sat down, one above the other, Albert below and Mary above.

It was there that he had given her a golden locket with a delicate chain. Their initials were entwined on the front surrounded by forget-me-nots.

"Oh, Albert! It's beautiful. It's the most wonderful gift I've ever been given."

"I had it made in Newport specially for you. Do you really like it?"

"Of course I do! Does it have your photograph inside?"

"Er, yes, it does," said Albert, his cheeks flushing immediately. "I can take it out if you would er, er...prefer something else."

"Oh, Albert, you haven't blushed or stuttered for simply ages. Help me put it on."

Mary turned around in the narrow space and lifted her hair away from her neck.

Once the locket was safely clasped, Mary turned around to face Albert.

"I won't be able to wear it at home, Albert, in case Aunt Sybil should see it, but I will make a little pouch for it and keep it close to my heart. You know what I need now, don't you?"

She pulled off his cap and ran her fingers through his hair.

"I need a lock of your hair. Shall I pull out a lock or two now?"

For an answer he had snatched back his cap and clattered away down the steps, laughing as he went.

As soon as Mary reached Boniface House after attending Sunday Morning Service with her aunt, uncle and sister she went straight upstairs, saying that she felt the need to lie down for a while. She refused the luncheon tray offered by her aunt even though she was hungry.

"Are you not feeling well?" asked Agnes when she came up to see what was wrong.

"I have a bad headache and think it would be best if I have a quiet afternoon. I won't go to Evensong."

"Would you like me to stay with you?"

"No, you go. I believe they will be singing a new arrangement of the Nunc Dimittis."

"Are you sure you will not come?"

Slightly disconcerted by her sister's unusual concern, Mary felt a momentary twinge of guilt for her falsehoods, but she carried on.

"Yes, quite sure. I will probably stay in bed for the rest of the day and hope to be recovered by the morning."

"I will ask Aunt Sybil to send Jane up to light your fire."

"No, that won't be necessary, I am quite warm. But thank you."

At half past three, Mary heard Dan start up the Humber and drive it round to the front of the house. She waited until she was sure that there had been no last-minute rushes back into the house for forgotten gloves or hymn books and then slipped out of bed, dressed quickly and pulled on her shoes. She retrieved Albert's book from her lingerie drawer and hurried downstairs to the deserted kitchen where she found some bread and cold meat to keep her hunger pangs at bay. Holding a sandwich in one hand and the book in the other, Mary hurried out of the house and ran towards the Landslip to meet Albert.

When she arrived, Albert was waiting for her, pacing back and forth in front of the Lovers' Seat. Without bothering to check that they were unobserved or even moving off the path a little way, Albert and Mary ran into each other's arms.

After a long embrace they moved slightly apart.

"You made it, then," he said, leaning forward again to kiss her cheek.

"Yes, I told you I would. I said I'd got a headache. How about you?"

"Nobody notices me very much, as long as I've done all my work."

"Oh, Albert!" she said.

They kissed.

"Albert! Stop!" she said, suddenly breaking away from him. "I have some important news."

"What is it?"

"Agnes and Gerald are engaged to be married. In October. But she doesn't love him, Albert, not properly, not as I love you. She was worried about becoming a spinster, that was all. She gave me a lecture and said I needed to find myself a suitable man and follow suit."

"I think neither your sister nor your aunt would consider me to be a suitable match."

"No, never, not even if your name wasn't de Versey!"

"What are we going to do, my dearest darling? I couldn't live without you."

"Don't worry! We will be together for always, I promise, but we must wait now until after Agnes is married – "

"But why wait until then?"

"Because if there was the slightest suggestion of impropriety on my part, Agnes's Gerald and his stuffy family would back out immediately. I couldn't have that on my conscience."

"Agnes doesn't deserve to have a sister such as you."

"She is sometimes a little unkind to me but I always remind myself that my birth turned her life completely topsy-turvey. To find yourself in a strange, cold country and with no parents or ayah must have been very shocking for a five-year-old child."

Albert put out his arms, drew Mary towards him and kissed her.

"I will never be unkind to you, dearest, darling Mary."

"Oh, Albert! I love you with all my heart."

Out for her usual Sunday evening walk with her spaniel, Miss Pryce's bunion began to trouble her so she decided to take a short cut through the Landslip instead of her usual route via the road. Dusk fell earlier in the Landslip because of all the overhanging trees and she was anxious to get home; she was looking forward to tea and toast with dripping from the Sunday joint.

"Come on, Floss, hurry up!"

Floss sat down and refused to move.

Standing quietly on the path waiting for her dog, Miss Pryce became aware of muffled voices and sounds coming from the clearing ahead. She dropped Floss's lead to the ground and moved noiselessly forward.

Chapter 7

With the boundary dispute settled in Sybil's favour, much to everyone's relief, early summer was a time of calm at Boniface House. Sybil did a grand tea time tour of neighbouring houses so she could tell everyone about her victory over the de Verseys, Agnes was busy with preparations for her wedding, Reginald had developed a passion for golf which kept him out of the house most days and Mary spent as much time as possible with Albert. Albert was excited because some of his poems were to be published in an anthology.

"There will be one especially for you, dearest Mary," he said as they walked slowly back to Bonchurch one sunny afternoon.

"Will you tell it to me now?"

"No, you must wait."

"How long must I wait?"

"Another month or two."

"How will I know which one it is?"

"It is a love poem. It starts out *When the world was born*, and there are three verses. I hope you will like it."

"I will love it."

Whilst things were calm at Boniface House, Miss Pryce had been getting steadily more annoyed at what she considered to be Sybil's condescending attitude.

"Going round the village as if she owns everything," she grumbled to Floss as she pulled down the Post Office shutters one evening. "And stopping us from walking down to the beach beside that old wall. We've been doing that for years, haven't we, Flossie."

The final straw for Miss Pryce came when Sybil telephoned the Post Office to dispute the bill for her daily newspaper delivery.

"Thinks I'm dishonest, does she, that pompous woman," she muttered, putting down the receiver. "We'll soon take her down a peg or two, shall we Floss?"

Chapter 8

"Where is Agnes?" Mary asked her aunt, coming into the drawing room through the French windows a few days later, unaware of the storm which awaited her. "It is a lovely afternoon and, look, I have picked her some foxgloves from along the lane."

Sybil was seated at her writing table. She did not look round.

"Agnes has gone over to the mainland to see Edwin and then she will be spending some time with her prospective parents-in-law."

"Oh, that is strange – she didn't say anything at lunch."

"I asked her not to speak of it. And I have sent your uncle up to London to see Leonard."

"Well, we shall be quiet. I'll go and change my clothes and be down again shortly. I am sorry if I missed tea," she added, catching sight of her aunt's angry face.

"It is too late for apologies, young lady. If missing tea was your only fault I should be much happier. Come here."

Mary put down the flowers and went to stand beside her aunt.

"It has come to my notice that you are currently the talk of Bonchurch with your scandalous behaviour."

"Me?"

"Yes, you. Quite scandalous. I hardly know how to speak of it. Have you no shame? Do you have no feeling for how such disgraceful behaviour reflects on this household? And with a de Versey! With a de Versey of all people! How could you! You know my feelings on that family. That my niece should be taken advantage of by a poor relation of theirs is beyond – "

"He has not taken advantage of me! Anything that has

happened between us has been with my full consent. And Albert might be poor but he is loyal and true and I love him!"

"Not only is he a poor relation of that dreadful family, he was also a conscientious objector during the war. How could you! A conchy! And a de Versey conchy. Your poor uncle would be horrified to think you could stoop so low."

"I don't mind what anyone thinks – "

"Oh, is that so? You will ruin this family for your own selfish desires? Have you no thought at all for Agnes? Or Edwin?"

"Of course I have – "

"Then you need to think what you are doing. I absolutely forbid you to see that man again."

"You can't forbid me!"

"Yes, I can. You forget, dear Mary, who holds the purse strings. I have been making plans since I discovered your guilty secret. Tonight, you and I will proceed immediately to London. We will stay at the Savoy overnight. The next evening you will board the night train for Baden Baden. I shall spend a day or two in London and return home with your uncle."

"But I don't want to go to Baden Baden!"

"If you refuse to co-operate I will have no hesitation in seeing to it that your sister's marriage does not go ahead, nor will I pay for your brother's articles which are due next month."

"Oh, you couldn't do that to Edwin and Agnes, Aunt Sybil, it would be too terrible. Uncle Reginald would never allow it."

"Your uncle is not here. And may I remind you who has paid for your education, your food, your clothing all these years? This is a banker's draft on Coutts," she continued, handing Mary a sheaf of papers. "You will find I have been more than generous – "

"I have never known you to be generous before, Aunt Sybil. It must have been very difficult for you."

"Please do not add insolence to your other faults. And this is the address of your pension in Baden Baden."

"I see. And when am I expected home?"

"When your health has returned."

"I assume that will be just before the wedding?"

"Yes. Let us hope that your notoriety will have abated by then. Jane has packed your bags; they are in the front hall. The taxi will be here within the hour. And do not think you can go running to Dan or Mrs Parsons and ask them to pass messages to that man for you – I have given them both two days holiday."

"Generous to a fault, Aunt Sybil."

"You will thank me for this one day – "

"Thank you? Thank you? I will never thank you, never, and I will never forgive you for what you are trying to do. Never, as long as I live."

"That's as may be. What is your decision?"

Chapter 9

Norfolk 1990

Jenny leant forwards and pulled the last box of books nearer to the sofa.

She picked up the slim volumes one by one, flipped through them, then put them down on one of the tottering reject piles or on the much smaller pile of books she wanted to keep. Most of the books had embossed leather or suede covers with gold lettering, some were spotted with age and had the pages roughly cut and several had tiny insect holes bored through from page to page. Jenny loved the ones with gold-edged, whisper thin leaves and marbled end papers, but she hadn't actually read many of them. They were old books, inherited from her Great Aunt Mary when she was a teenager. Some years ago, she had checked on the internet to see if any of them were valuable but they were nothing more than her great aunt's eclectic mix of classical authors, poetry and prose.

Besides the books, Jenny had inherited three framed watercolours painted by her great aunt, and her sketchbook. Her sister, Sue, had inherited their great aunt's jewellery.

"It's mostly costume jewellery, Jenny," Sue had said, "so don't get upset. You know she loved us both and I expect she thought you'd like the books and paintings more than her bits and pieces. You can have the owl brooch if you want."

"No, it's OK, you keep the brooch and I'll remember her by the books and sketches. Thanks, anyway."

And now the books were going. Geoff had taken over the dining room where the books had been kept and there was no space in the sitting room, so Great Aunt Mary's books were on their way to a charity shop.

She and Geoff had had a bit of an argument about his appropriation of the dining room.

"We'll never use it now the kids have gone to uni," he said, "and I can't fit anything else into that little bedroom – I want a proper office."

Jenny had other plans. She wanted to take up painting again and bring in her equipment from the garage where it had lain untouched for a few years. Living with teenaged twins as they went through their exams, their gap year and preparing for university hadn't left her much time for watercolours. Now she wanted to take up oil painting and had already ear-marked a possible evening class.

"But what about my painting?" she said. "I want to use the dining room because it's got lovely light in the mornings. And my things wouldn't take up so much space so there'd still be enough room for a dining table."

"Can't you clear a bit of space in the kitchen?"

"No, I need to be able to leave my things out, not put them away every time we sit down to eat."

"But you won't be doing so much cooking now it's just you and me."

"Ben and Megan haven't gone for good, they'll be back for the holidays and you and I still need to be able to sit down somewhere."

"Come on, Jenny! I can't possibly work in the kitchen. Anyway, I've ordered a new desk and chair. They're coming next week."

And that was that.

Jenny looked into the box of books – another twenty or so to go and then it would be done. She reached down and picked up another volume. It was slimmer than most of the others with a maroon leather cover and a silken bookmark. She turned it over in her hand and then lifted it to her nose. It didn't smell fusty like the rest. As she held it in her hand, it opened at the bookmark to reveal a poem with what looked like her aunt's writing at the end. Jenny lifted it up to the light. Written with a soft leaded pencil were the words *Forever in My Heart* and her great aunt's initials, M.F.B., Mary Frances Bennett. It was a love poem.

For a long time, Jenny sat on the sofa with the book on her lap, trying to imagine her spinster great aunt with a sweetheart who wrote poems. Or maybe it wasn't a lover, just a poem she liked. Or nothing at all to do with Great Aunt Mary and the initials were simply a coincidence? Was it even her writing?

Engrossed in her thoughts, Jenny didn't hear Geoff's car on the drive and she jumped when the front door slammed. Without thinking what she was doing, she pushed the book behind the sofa cushion and leant against it.

"Haven't you finished those books yet?" asked Geoff as he came into the sitting room.

"No, not yet."

"I'm getting fed up with the mess – they've been hanging around for ages. I suppose you haven't found any first editions or £50 notes tucked away?"

"No, nothing. Just old books."

"I'm off out tonight – "

"Again? You've been out twice this week already."

"Yes, I know, that's how it goes. I'll grab myself something to eat. Be back around eleven. Don't wait up."

Jenny listened to her husband's movements as he went upstairs, came down again and went into the kitchen. She heard the fridge door open and close and imagined rather than heard the click and whoosh as he opened a can of beer. There was silence for a while, then the back door opened as he went outside for a cigarette. Only when Jenny heard the front door slam again and his car go up the drive did she retrieve the book from behind the cushion and read the poem.

When the World was Born

When the world was born
So our love was written, prophesised,
Created as the morning star
As constant as the dawn.
You are beauty's envy
My heart's delight.

As fruit ripens on the bough,
And all things come to pass.
So passion's urges shall be met.
My love, say it will be now!
You are beauty's envy
My heart's delight.

And when the world is old
Our love will sing its song
Whispered in the stars
And never will grow cold.
You are beauty's envy
My heart's delight.

Albert de Versey

Chapter 10

"Hi, Jen. What's up? Why are you ringing so early?"

"Morning, Sue. Nothing's up, I just didn't sleep well, one of those nights, and I wanted to talk to you."

"What about?"

"Great Aunt Mary."

"Great Aunt Mary?"

"Yes. You know I'm trying to sort out her books now Geoff has got the dining room?"

"That wasn't right, Jen, you should have stood up to him a bit more. It's your house as well."

"Mm, yes, I know, but it's too late now. Anyway, have you got any old letters from Great Aunt Mary?"

"Letters?"

"Yes, Sue, letters, those things the postman brings."

"OK, no need to be snarky. I'm hardly awake."

"Sorry. Have you got any? I know I haven't."

"I don't think so. Why do you want them?"

"I need to check out her handwriting."

"Why on earth do you want to check her handwriting?"

Jenny explained about finding what could be their aunt's writing in one of the old books.

"After a love poem?"

"Yes. Written by an Albert de Versey."

"Never heard of him."

"No, neither have I. I found a Walter de Versey when I had a quick look on the internet last night, he was quite famous, but not an Albert. If I know it's her writing, I'll do some more research and see if Walter had a brother. Can you look for some of her letters?"

"I'll try but I'm not hopeful. I had a big turn-out when we

moved down here."

"Oh, I wish you hadn't moved so far away! I miss you."

"Now your Megan and Ben are at uni why don't you come down for a long weekend?"

"I'll try. I miss them, too."

"How are they getting on?"

"No idea – neither of them has rung."

"Well, that's pretty normal. Don't worry, Jen, they'll be fine. Do you remember when Beth went and I nearly sent out a search party? I'll see what I can do about any letters."

"Thanks, Sue, you're an angel."

"Yes, I know. I've got a surgery this morning but I'm off this afternoon so I'll have a look then. If I've got any I'll post them to you tonight. Bye, Jen!"

By the time Jenny had finished on the phone, Geoff was downstairs and eating his breakfast in the kitchen.

"You're up early," he said, without looking up from the paper.

"Yes, couldn't sleep."

"Who were you talking to?"

"Sue."

"She okay?"

"Yes, fine."

Jenny poured herself some coffee and sat down. Geoff was wearing his good suit and she could smell his aftershave.

"You in court today?"

"Yes," he said. "Ipswich."

He buttered his toast then reached out for the marmalade.

"You were late last night," she said.

"Yes, couldn't get away."

"I finished the books while you were out, so can you carry the boxes out to my car? There's three of them."

"OK." He looked at her over the top of the paper. "Do you want me to take them in mine? Save your back unloading?"

"Oh, thanks, that'd be good."

Jenny had decided not to talk to him about the Great Aunt Mary book or the poem. She knew he would be able to tell her exactly how to go about finding an Albert de Versey, or probably get someone from the office to do it for her, but she didn't want that. It was going to be private. Her secret.

As soon as he'd gone, Jenny unloaded the dishwasher, cleared away the breakfast things and then went to fetch the book from its hiding place in her bedside drawer.

She sat down on the edge of the bed and flipped through the book once more. There were contributions from various poets and authors she had heard of but there were no more poems by an Albert de Versey. It was still possible that the pencilled writing was nothing more than someone else's thoughtless scribble, but Jenny knew that, if it was her great aunt's writing, the writing on that particular page was important. Great Aunt Mary would never write in books without a good reason. The more she looked at the pencilled writing the more convinced she became that the poem was written specially for her aunt.

Chapter II

When Sue and Jenny were small their mother took them to visit their grandparents twice a year, at Easter and Christmas. They enjoyed the journey because it involved a slow train into London then an underground to Waterloo where their mother would let them buy comics and sweets from the bookstall.

"Don't forget to save some sweets for later," she would say as she settled down on a bench with her Prima magazine to wait for the Dorking train. "You'll need them to take away the taste of another one of your grandmother's delicious gooseberry suet puddings!"

It wasn't only the cooking which Sue and Jenny didn't like. The house was large but uncomfortable and cold. Their grandfather spent most of the time on the golf course or in his study, only appearing at meal times, and their grandmother most certainly wasn't the warm and loving sort. She checked their teeth, their heights, their reading and spelling abilities and she always frowned at their clothes.

"When I was a girl, trousers were not thought suitable attire for young ladies," she said. "Did you not pack them any dresses at all, Imogen? Not even for church on Easter morning?".

"No. They don't like dresses."

"Well, have you taught them to sew, yet?"

"No. They don't like sewing. Or knitting, before you ask."

"They are very useful skills – "

"Not for my girls they're not. Sue's doing really well at her sciences and Jenny won the art prize at school last year. Going to do it again this year, aren't you Jen." She ruffled her daughter's hair. "Come on, you two, let's go out for a walk."

Long walks up over the Surrey hills with their mother and occasional trips by train to the sea at Worthing made the Easter visit bearable for the two children. At Christmas there was a decorated tree in the hallway and presents on Christmas day but, for Sue and Jenny, the highlight of the holiday was spending time with Great Aunt Mary. The day before Christmas Eve their mother borrowed her father's car and they would collect her from the coach station. Great Aunt Mary was always the last one off the Oxford coach, trailing drapes and scarves, her hair falling out of the loose bun at the nape of her neck and with a leather shoulder bag slung around her shoulders. Jenny remembered the warmth of her mother and Great Aunt Mary's reunion as they kissed, hugged and laughed together, a show of affection never seen between their mother and grandmother, Agnes.

As soon as she was in the car, bringing with her the familiar smell of 4711 stick cologne, Great Aunt Mary rummaged around in one or other of the bags at her feet and eventually, when Sue and Jenny were on tenterhooks, she handed over a big paper bag full of toffee whirls.

"Don't eat them all at once," she would say, "and don't tell your grandmother or I shall get into trouble."

As soon as they were back at Lansdowne House and all the luggage had been brought in from the car, there would be a tray of tea and mince pies waiting for them in the sitting room.

"How have you been keeping, Mary?" asked Agnes once everyone was settled. "Did you receive my last letter telling you about Edwin's Connie?

"Oh, I knew about that already – she wrote and told me. Edwin would have been very proud. My health is good. How are you, Agnes?"

"My vertigo does not improve. Will you have another mince pie?"

"Oh, no, not for me. Here we are girls, you can have the

rest," she said, holding the plate out to Sue and Jenny. "I know you two just love your grandmother's mince pies."

Their mother coughed and stood up as Sue and Jenny tried to stifle their giggles.

"Well, if everyone's finished I'll take the tray out to the kitchen. Sue and Jenny, why don't you help Grammy carry her bags upstairs. Go on, off you go."

If their grandmother came into the room whenever Great Aunt Mary, Jenny and Sue and their mother were playing Christmas games, Mary would stop laughing and stare at her sister, as if daring her to interrupt. Agnes would continue into the room, straighten the curtains, check that the fire wasn't burning too fiercely or plump up the cushions and then go out again. As soon as Agnes was out of the room, her sister would get up, put more coal on the fire and sit down on top of one of the cushions. She then winked at their mother and they would both laugh.

"Mum, don't Grandma and Grammy like each other?" Jenny asked one evening as her mother was putting her to bed.

"Sisters don't always get on together, darling."

"But I love Sue."

"Yes. She loves you, too."

"Why aren't they like us?"

"I don't really know. Don't forget what I told you about their parents dying when your Great Uncle Edwin, Grandma and Grammy were very young. Grammy was only a baby. They had to go and live with your Great Great Aunt Sybil and so they didn't have a very happy childhood. Maybe it's something to do with that."

"Is Great Great Aunt Sybil that grumpy one in the Isle of Wight? She told me off for something when we went there once."

"Yes, that's the one. You were only very little and you pulled all the croquet hoops out of the lawn."

"I wish Grammy was our grandmother instead of

Grandma."

"Mm, yes. When I was little I always wanted her as my mother but that's not how it was. Now, lie down and try to get to sleep."

"Mum, why can't Grammy come and live with us?"

"She loves her little house in Oxford and we haven't really got room."

"No, s'pose not. When's Sue coming up?"

"She'll be up shortly. Good night sweetheart."

Chapter 12

When the promised letter arrived from Sue on Saturday morning, it was not a bulky A4 envelope full of Great Aunt Mary's letters as Jenny had hoped. It contained a single sheet of paper from Sue and one of her old birthday cards from Grammy.

Darling Jen,

I'm afraid this is all I could find. It's the last birthday card she sent, which is probably why I kept it. Probably not much good for checking her handwriting. But last Christmas I had a card from Great Uncle Edwin's daughter, Connie. Do you remember her? She came to Mum's funeral. She'd heard somehow that I'd moved down here and wanted to get in touch. We met for an hour or so in Bournemouth a couple of months ago. She's elderly and a bit frail but totally with it. Very sweet. I don't suppose she'd have any of Grammy's handwriting, but she might know whether Grammy ever had a poet boyfriend. She might even know why Grammy and Grandma were always at daggers drawn. They were always so secretive! Something must have happened.
Anyway, why don't you come down here for a long weekend and we could go and see her? She lives in Boscombe.

Love and kisses,

Sue

P.S. She gave me a photo of a house in the I of W which she thinks is where her father, Grandma and Grammy grew up.
XXX

Jenny studied the old birthday card. Sue was right – the writing was wavery and all over the place, an old woman's writing. It was nothing like *Forever in My Heart* in the old book. She propped up the card on the mantelpiece and went to make herself some coffee. Geoff would be back from golf at lunchtime so she had an hour or so to try and do a bit more research on Walter de Versey. If she found Walter's date of birth, she could look for him on the 1891 census and see if he had a brother called Albert. There was still a computer in Geoff's old upstairs office but it was very slow so she decided to use his new Apple Mac. She took her coffee to his office and settled down in his chair. He had wanted to put a lock on the door once he had changed the room from dining room to office until Jenny complained.

"But suppose someone broke in and stole all my files or the computer? It's a top of the range model."

"Geoff, we have locks on all the windows and doors and a burglar alarm. Anyway, I'm not having a locked room in my own home."

Jenny had helped him to set up the computer so she remembered his password – nothing to do with her or their children, it was his mother's maiden name followed by the registration number of his first car, freedland RGO103. RGO 103 was a pale blue Triumph Mayflower which he had been driving when they first met, not like the students at her art college who drove Isetta bubble cars, mopeds or clapped-out vans. Geoff had brought her flowers and taken her out to expensive restaurants rather than down the local chippie.

Jenny's mother encouraged their romance because she wanted to see her young daughter settled before she died.

Jenny dropped out of the last year of her arts degree and she and Geoff were married a few months before her mother died of breast cancer. As soon as he secured his second training contract, Geoff had swapped the Triumph for an old Jaguar XJ6. When the twins were born, he had to downgrade to an estate car which upset him no end. Jenny smiled at the memory. She typed in the password.

Geoff hadn't shut down the computer properly so the first thing which came up was what he had been working on the night before.

It was not to do with work. It was an email.

'Darling Brigitte.'

For a few moments Jenny sat and stared at the computer screen without being able to read any more. She took a deep breath to try to quell the rising tide of panic which threatened to engulf her. Oh, surely, please no, not again! Her first instinct was to try and forget what she had seen, close the computer, go out of his office and pretend everything was still the same. She pushed back the chair and tried to stand up but her legs gave way.

When the twins were toddlers and Jenny was exhausted with endless sleepless nights and tantrum-filled days, Geoff had an affair with a new secretary at the office. When one of the senior partners found out what was going on Geoff was told to finish the affair at once or lose his job. He chose his job. Jenny didn't find out until some years later when Geoff told her what had happened.

"It was when you were so busy with the twins. You hardly knew I was there."

"If you'd helped out a bit more I wouldn't have been so busy, so don't you dare put all the blame on me. It was you who had the affair. It was you, not me."

"I'm truly sorry, Jen. It was a terrible thing to do but – "

"There are no buts. What you did when I needed you

most was a terrible thing to do. Inexcusable."

"Yes, but – "

"Geoff!"

"No, you're right. Inexcusable. Sorry. It will never happen again. Promise."

Jenny had forgiven him and they worked together to make a good life for themselves, Megan and Ben. Until now.

Maybe it wasn't as bad as she thought. Maybe the 'Darling' was a mistake and he hadn't been concentrating. But who was Brigitte and why was Geoff writing to her? Where did she live? Jenny risked a quick look at the text. No address. How had he signed off? She scrolled to the bottom of the page. The email was unfinished. She remembered that last night, when she went into the office to tell him Megan had rung at last, Geoff immediately stood up from the computer. He came to the front of his desk and then went with her out to the kitchen with his arm around her shoulder. They'd had a glass of wine together.

Jenny stared at the computer screen. Geoff had promised it would never happen again so the 'Darling' must be a mistake, something easily explained. She decided it would be best to read what he had written and set her mind at rest, then get on with researching Walter de Versey before Geoff came home. She drank some of her cooling coffee and started to read.

It wasn't good. Geoff was acting as Brigitte's divorce lawyer. There was nothing sexually implicit like the toe-curling Camillagate tapes which had been all over the papers recently, but it was certainly not a disinterested email from a solicitor to a client and the Darling was not a mistake. He was making arrangements to take her to see *A Little Light Music* at the National. Bastard.

She read through the text once more, sat for a long time in silence with her eyes shut, then printed out a copy. She left his computer as she had found it, turned off the printer, picked up her coffee mug and went out of the room, shutting the door behind her. She went into the sitting room, folded the A4 sheet into quarters and slipped it into one of Grammy's books – A Shell Guide to the Isle of Wight by Pennethorne Hughes. Grammy would look after it for her until she decided what to do.

When Geoff came back from his golf, Jenny was in the kitchen preparing a salad.

"Good game?" she asked.

Chapter 13

For several days, Jenny did nothing. Geoff came and went as usual and Jenny tried to find out a bit more about Albert using the old upstairs computer, rather than the Apple Mac. It was difficult to concentrate as her mind kept returning to the letter hidden in Great Aunt Mary's book. She thought about the life she and Geoff had lived and what she would do if he had been unfaithful. She clung to the hope that nothing much had happened. Surely, he had enough good sense not to risk his marriage and career again. He was hoping to be made a full partner in the autumn and an affair with one of his clients would not go down well. For once in her life, she felt she had some power over Geoff. He didn't know what she knew and that felt good and rather exciting.

The confrontation was not long in coming.

"Oh, Jen, I forgot to tell you," said Geoff when he came home from work unexpectedly early one evening. "There's a do at work next week. Mainly social, you know the type of thing, and I need you to come with me."

"What day?"

"Thursday."

"But that's the day of my new painting class and I don't want to miss the first one." Jenny put down her book and looked at him. "Anyway, what sort of social and why have I got to come?"

"All the partners and their wives are going to be there and I want to make a good impression." He handed her a glass of wine.

"But they already know me. I don't need to be scrutinised."

"I know, but this one is important."

"Why?"

"It's Kerridge's birthday and he's going to announce his retirement. I think final decisions are going to be made on me being made a full partner. I really need you there to show that my family life is all hunky dory."

Jenny took a large mouthful of wine and swallowed it slowly.

"Is it?"

"Is it what?"

"Hunky dory?"

"What could be better? A beautiful wife, lovely home, two fantastic kids at university, no money problems. All hunky dory." He bent down and kissed the top of her head.

It was the kiss on top of her head rather than her cheek or her mouth which suddenly enraged Jenny. She watched as Geoff turned away and put his wine glass down on the table. His hand was shaking slightly. She sat up straighter and took a deep breath.

"Why don't you take Brigitte?"

Later that evening, after Geoff had disappeared off to the Golf Club, Jenny sat down in the kitchen and thought for a long time about what to do. Once her mind was made up, she rang her sister.

"What's up Jen? You don't usually ring this late."

"Can I come down to yours for that long weekend we talked about?"

"Why do you want to come now?" asked Sue. "You didn't sound extra keen last week. 'I'll try' is what you said."

"Yes, but things have changed a bit and I need to get away for a while."

"Get away? Why? What on earth's happened? You're not ill, are you?"

"No, no, nothing like that but I need to get away."

"Of course you can come here. Jen, you sound really upset – is it something to do with Geoff?"

"I'll tell you when I see you."

"He's not hurt you, has he?"

"No, course not. Can I come tomorrow?"

"Course you can. Train or car?"

"Car, then I can get over to the Isle of Wight and do a bit of research on the de Verseys at the same time."

"You still on that?"

"Yes, really interesting. Can we visit that Connie woman?"

"Great Uncle Edwin's Connie?"

"Yes, her."

"I should think so. How long are you going to stay?"

"Until I decide what to do."

"It is Geoff, isn't it."

"Oh, Sue, I really can't talk now, it's too difficult. I'll tell you when I see you. Tomorrow afternoon, then?"

"Do you want me to come up and fetch you?"

"No, I'll be OK."

"Sure?"

"Yes."

"OK. Drive carefully."

"I will. Bye."

In the early hours of the morning, she heard Geoff's tread on the stairs. She watched as the bedroom door handle turned slowly. He came a little way into the bedroom, stopped, and looked at her.

"What do you want?" she asked.

"Oh, Jen! Please believe me. I promise you, I promise! I've told you, nothing's happened, nothing at all. She's just a very needy client."

"One you call darling and take to the theatre?"

"She bought the tickets and I couldn't say no."

"Yes, you could."

Turning away, he saw her packed bag on the floor beside

the bed.
"Are you going away?"
"Yes."
"Where?"
"Shut the door."
"But when will you come back?"
"Go away and shut the door."

Chapter 14

The next morning, Jenny woke at first light from a fitful sleep. She showered, dressed, gathered her belongings and went quietly down the stairs. Geoff was stretched out on the sofa, still in his clothes. She went straight to the kitchen to collect her car keys. At the front door, she paused and looked back at Geoff. He hadn't stirred, but when she drove away he was standing by the window watching her. He raised his hand in salute. She nodded her head slightly in acknowledgement.

"Oh, Jen! You look terrible!" said Sue, when Jenny arrived at her sister's house mid-morning.

"Thanks."

"Was it a tiring journey?"

"Not too bad. Where are Zip and Fly?" Jenny asked, looking round for the two border terriers who usually bounded out to greet her.

"They're with Duncan. Come on, in you come." She picked up her sister's bag. "I've made us a salad and jacket potatoes for lunch."

"I'm not that hungry."

"You'll manage a bit of salad."

"Bossy-boots, as ever."

They both started to laugh but Jenny's laughter turned quickly to tears and sobs.

"Oh, I'm sorry!" said Jenny, disentangling herself from her sister's arms once she had stopped crying. "There's snot all over your top."

"Not to worry, you always were a bit of a dribbler. How about a quick G & T before I force you to eat some salad? And there's someone in the kitchen I want you to meet. Come on."

"I can't meet anyone, not like this!"

"Flora won't mind."

Sue took hold of her sister's hand and drew her towards the kitchen.

"Don't make too much noise, she's still a bit frightened."

She opened the door slowly, pulled her sister into the room and then closed the door quietly behind them.

"There she is! Duncan brought her home a few days ago. She was found wandering around Lymington half-starved and there wasn't any room at the clinic so he brought her home, as per usual."

But Jenny wasn't listening; she was on the floor beside the dog's bed, running her hand along the knobbly spine and looking into the dog's eyes.

"She's so thin! Oh, look, Sue! She's wagging her tail. Poor thing, has no-one been loving you? Who named her Flora?" Jenny asked, turning to look at her sister.

"Me. That's the first thing she did – took a whole tub of Flora off the kitchen table and ate the lot."

"Poor girl. Were you hungry, then? I hope you weren't sick."

"Yes, she was. All over everywhere. Thank heavens for washing machines. Blood, sweat, tears and sick – this house is frequently full of it. Not to mention wee," she added, looking at Flora.

"Well, if you will marry a vet and have a weepy sister, what can you expect?"

It wasn't until the next morning, with a cup of coffee in front of her and Flora at her feet, that Jenny felt able to tell her sister what had happened.

"Do you believe him? That nothing's been going on?"

"I want to. I'm hoping that he wouldn't have been so stupid. He really loves his job and I can't see him jeopardising that, but there was that other time."

"Mm, yes. That was awful."

"It's nearly sixteen years ago now."

"How old is this Brigitte?"

"No idea."

"Could you do a little digging? Find out her surname? If she's using Geoff's firm for her divorce she can't be short of a bob or two so there might be something about her on the internet. Is she English?"

"No idea."

"Do Ben and Megan know where you are?"

"I got hold of Meggie but not Ben."

"Hasn't he rung at all, yet?"

"No. Megan said she'd get on to him."

"Come on, finish up your coffee and we'll take Flora down to the river for a walk. Duncan said she could probably manage a short one and you look as if you could do with a bit of fresh air as well."

"OK. I've done enough thinking about what's happened, now I'd rather think about Grammy instead. I've brought the book with me so you can see the writing when we get back. I'm sure it's her."

"Come on, Flora, walkies time," said Sue. She stood up but Flora didn't move, her head still resting against Jenny's leg.

"Oh, Sue! She doesn't know what that means! Zip and Fly would be waiting at the door by now." She reached down to fondle the dog's ears.

"Duncan said her claws were overgrown so she'd probably been kept shut up somewhere."

"How old is she?"

"He thinks she's under a year, so she might have been a Christmas puppy that grew up."

"Poor dog. Never mind, you're in a good place now. Come on, girlie, up you get."

Flora, Sue and Jenny enjoyed their slow walk beside the river and Jenny felt able to relax for the first time since she'd found the Brigitte letter. By the time Duncan came home to Buckthorn House with the terriers, Jenny and Sue had decided that *Forever in my Heart* written in the anthology next to Albert de Versey's poem was definitely in their great aunt's handwriting. Sue had suggested that Jenny could hire a historian to find out a bit more about Albert and Jenny had immediately fixed up an appointment with a man from a historical society on the Isle of Wight.

"When are you going to meet him?" Duncan asked.

"He's free tomorrow afternoon, so I've booked an early ferry crossing to Yarmouth and a hotel in Ventnor for a couple of days. His name's Henry Thirlby. He sounded pretty ancient and he had a terrible cough, but he thought he could help."

"Let's hope so. Glass of wine, anyone?"

Chapter 15

The hotel in Ventnor was right on the sea front, approached via a steeply zig-zagging road. Jenny booked herself in, took her overnight bag up to her room and then went out for a quick look around and something to eat before meeting Henry Thirlby. It was getting towards the end of the season, so the town wasn't too busy and Jenny enjoyed strolling around on her own without having to worry about keeping Geoff waiting anywhere or trying to find a proper restaurant for lunch. She bought herself an ice cream, then followed it up with a bag of chips which she ate on a bench beside the children's paddling pool. She smiled to herself as she imagined what Geoff might say about her choice of food.

By two o'clock she was ready and waiting in the café up at the Winter Gardens where Henry Thirlby had suggested they meet. At half past two she was on her second pot of tea and wondering how much longer she should wait, when a young man rushed in and scanned the room, obviously looking for someone. When he saw Jenny sitting on her own, he came straight over.

"Hi! So sorry to keep you waiting. You are Jenny Holmes, aren't you?"

"Yes, that's me."

"Thank goodness you're still here. Grandad forgot to tell me about you."

"Grandad?"

"Yes, sorry, it's all been a bit of a rush. He was taken into hospital last night with pneumonia and he only told me about you when I went to visit him."

He pulled out a chair and sat down opposite Jenny then quickly stood again and held out his hand.

"So sorry, I should've have introduced myself. I'm Theo, Henry's grandson."

His hand shake was firm and warm. Jenny smiled at him and motioned him back to his chair.

"Is that tea in the pot?" he asked. "I'm desperate."

Jenny poured him out a cup. She watched as he added three heaped spoons of sugar, stirred it round then drank it all off.

"Phew, that's better. Haven't had time for anything today."

"I'm sorry to hear about your grandfather. How is he?"

"He's a tough old stick. Hope he'll be home soon."

"It was your grandfather I was hoping to see."

"Yes, I know, I've been living with him for a while so I was there when you rang yesterday. Something about an Albert de Vesty?"

"Versey, Albert de Versey. Your grandfather said he might be able to find out whether Albert had any connections to the Isle of Wight. My great aunt might have known him."

"There's not much Grandad doesn't know about the Isle of Wight, and I've just finished an M.A. in family history, so between us we should be able to help you."

He grinned at her and Jenny smiled back.

"I've got this book," she said, pushing it across the table to him, "and there's a poem in it written by Albert de Versey."

He took the book into his hand, stroked the maroon leather cover and then held it to his nose and breathed in deeply, exactly as she had done.

"Page 56, it's on page 56, with the peacock bookmark."

"What's the writing?" he asked, peering sideways at the lettering.

"It says *Forever in my Heart* and MFB are my great aunt's initials."

"Interesting."

There was silence for a while as he read the poem.

"Were they lovers?"

"I don't know. As far as I know, my great aunt never married. She and my grandmother would never talk about the past. Any questions about their youth were strictly out of bounds."

"It's a very sweet little love poem. Shame if they didn't get together."

"Yes. I think something awful must have happened but I don't know what. A relation gave my sister this photograph and we think the house might be where they were brought up. My sister can remember going to a big house where there were servants' bells in the kitchen and a croquet lawn."

"I love photographs! They tell you so much. I should think this is about the turn of the century judging by the clothes."

"The three children in the front are our great uncle Edwin, our grandmother Agnes and that little dark-haired one on the end is our great aunt Mary, but there's nothing on the back to say where it was taken or who the other people are."

Theo groaned.

"Oh, I wish people would document things properly, it'd make things so much easier. What was your great aunt's surname?"

"Bennett. She was Mary Frances Bennett and she was born around 1901 or 1902."

"OK, I'll see what I can do. A house somewhere near Ventnor you said?"

"Yes."

"I'll take the photo to show the old man, he might recognise it, and I'll do some research on Albert and your great aunt. I'll be in touch as soon as I've got any news. Where are you staying?"

"At the Clifton, down on the sea front. Do you think you'll be able to find anything?" Jenny asked.

"I should think so. Do you know the hotel phone number?"

"No, I don't but I'm sure it'll be in the book. Or you could try ringing me on my mobile phone, it should work here."

"A mobile phone?"

"Yes. The number is 07635 821821."

Theo pulled out a dog-eared notebook and scribbled down the number.

"I'll get one soon," he said. "They must be handy. Save a lot of time looking for phone boxes."

"Yes," she laughed, "and for keeping in touch with errant children."

"Yeah, good for that, too. I'll get going, then."

He stood up, reached across the table, shook her hand again and turned to go.

"The photograph! Don't forget that."

"Sorry, thinking about Grandad. I'll be in touch."

Jenny watched as he hurried through the tables and chairs, waved to the waiter and disappeared out of the door.

When Jenny got back to the Clifton, the receptionist beckoned her over.

"There's a message for you, Mrs Holmes."

He looked down at the papers on his desk.

"Yes, that's right, it was your sister. She would like you to call her."

As soon as she was back in her room, she dialled Sue's number.

"Ah, there you are at last. I've been trying reach you on your mobile."

"It's been turned off. Is everything OK?"

"Yes, everything's OK but Geoff rang and I promised him I'd tell you he's been trying to talk to you. I didn't tell him where you are. He sounded pretty awful. Anyway, at least you know he's been trying to talk to you. Tell me, how did you get on with the researcher?"

"Well, it wasn't him, it was his grandson because the

grandfather's in hospital with pneumonia. Grandson Theo is going to see what he can find out about Albert. He took the house photo to show his grandfather. I expect he'll ring tomorrow."

"Are you going to ring Geoff?"

"No, I don't think so, not yet."

"You OK?"

"Yes, pretty good. Thanks, Sue. I'll ring you tomorrow morning. Bye."

As soon as she replaced the receiver, Jenny felt a sudden wave of unhappiness sweep over her. She was tempted to ring Sue back to talk for a bit longer but she sat quietly for a while then blew her nose, swung her legs over the edge of the bed and went to the window. The sun was out, the sea was calm and there were still people on the beach, so she decided to go down and have a paddle to cheer herself up before going into the town to find something to eat. If it was fine again tomorrow, she would buy a swimsuit and make the time for a quick dip. She changed into shorts and a tee shirt and made her way downstairs.

The water was warmer than she expected and the tide was on the turn so there was plenty of firm sand to walk on and gentle waves to jump over. She rolled up her shorts and went deeper and deeper. She laughed with delight when a bigger than expected wave whooshed up her back. Realising she was nearly wet all over, she decided she might as well have a swim and be done with it. She turned her back on the shore, waded out a bit deeper and dived into the next wave. When she came back, her sandals and towel were only just beyond the reach of the incoming tide. She tied the towel round her wet shorts, slipped her sandy feet into the waiting sandals and made her way back to the hotel. After a shower, she rinsed out her salty clothes and draped them over the bath and was about to have a quick rest on the bed when she realised how hungry she was.

It was still quite early in the evening but she really fancied a large glass of wine and lasagne with chips as a side, rather than a healthy salad. Another thing Geoff would have disapproved of, never mind swimming in her clothes.

She wandered around Ventnor looking for somewhere to eat until the sound of music and laughter drew her towards a small pub up a side street. The menu outside wasn't particularly special but she went in, ordered lasagne and chips, and took a glass of wine to a corner table. She was on her second glass before the food arrived. The lasagne looked rather greasy and the chips were overcooked but she didn't mind. She was half-way through her meal when a crowd of young people came in, talking and laughing together, and she noticed Theo amongst them. She raised her hand and smiled at him. He left his friends and came over.

"Hi, good to see you. Not much further on with Albert and your great aunt, I'm afraid."

"Yes, good to see you, too. Don't worry, I wasn't expecting any news tonight. How is your grandfather?"

"He was asleep when I visited so I couldn't show him the photo. I left it on his bedside locker so he'll see it in the morning."

"Can I get you a drink? Or something to eat? Are you hungry?" she asked when she saw Theo eyeing her chips.

"I'm starving. Haven't had time to get myself anything. Was going to get fish and chips later, but if you're offering?"

"Certainly am. Will your friends mind you deserting them?"

"No, I don't think they'll miss me."

"Go and get yourself a drink, then, and order whatever you want to eat."

"Thanks. There were a couple of things I forgot to ask so we can eat and talk."

"If you drink wine, how about getting a bottle?"

"OK. Won't be long."

Jenny watched as he went over to his group of friends, took his leave of them, then went to the bar. The barman greeted him by name and he was served quickly.

"A friend of yours?" she asked, nodding towards the barman, as Theo sat down next to her.

"Yeah, he's a good mate. We were at university together a couple of years ago. He'll hustle up the food."

"I've got twins and they've just started at uni. One at Brighton, one at Warwick."

By the time Theo's food arrived, Jenny was laughing as Theo told her about some of his early days at university.

"I'm hoping to go on and do a doctorate," he said, "and I was offered a place at Oxford but a relationship went wrong and then Grandad needed someone to stay near him for a while, so, here I am."

"Nothing here on the Island?"

"No. I've deferred for a year."

He poured her out more wine and began to eat.

"Do you want something else?" she asked when his plate was empty.

"Yeah, still a few holes to fill. You going to have something?"

"Why not?"

By the time they had finished the food, another bottle of wine and a couple of brandies each, they were enjoying each other's company and didn't realise they were the last people in the pub until the barman called goodnight to Theo as he went off shift.

"I'll walk with you to the Clifton, it's on my way," said Theo as Jenny came back from paying the bill. "Haven't you got a coat or a jacket or something? Forecast's bad and the wind's got up."

"No, but it's not far."

"Come on, then, let's make a dash for it."

They went out into the street. Theo took her hand and

they ran down to the sea front together, laughing as they were buffeted by the onshore wind.

"Thanks for a lovely evening," said Jenny when they reached the Clifton. "Haven't had so much fun for ages."

"Yeah, it was good. I'll ring you tomorrow."

He stood and looked at her for a moment then took both her hands in his, leant forward and kissed her cheek.

"Yes," he said, "it was good."

Chapter 16

The next morning, Jenny's head was aching and she didn't feel like sitting in the dining room surrounded by people eating fried breakfasts, so she took some coffee and toast to a low table at the front of the hotel looking out over the sea.

She was on her second cup of coffee when she saw a battered Mini come to an abrupt halt outside. Theo leapt out, slammed the car door and ran up the steps into the hotel. She went to meet him.

"Jenny! I've got some news."

"About Albert?"

"No, no, it's the house. Grandad rang me this morning from the hospital and he knows where it is, it's in Upper Bonchurch. He says it's now one of those fancy hotels, called The Boniface. Do you want to go and look?"

"Now?"

"Yes, now. This afternoon I'm going to Newport Records Office to do a bit of research on your Albert de Versey, then I want to go and see how Grandad is doing."

"I'll get my jacket."

As she went up to her room, Jenny was glad there hadn't been time for any awkwardness about last night's kiss. During the night she had decided it was probably just a young man's way of thanking her for the food and drink. He would have had no way of knowing how the look in his eyes, the feel of his hands and the touch of his lips on her cheek had made her feel.

She grabbed her jacket, bag and camera and hurried down the stairs.

"Come on, the car's out front. It won't take long to get there."

He took hold of her hand to hurry her along.

Jenny had sat with both Megan and Ben as they learnt to drive, but nothing could have prepared her for Theo's driving as he rocketed up and down steep hills and shot round hairpin bends.

"Can you slow down a bit?" she asked, as they careered towards another corner.

"Feeling a little delicate, are you?" he asked with a grin, turning to look at her instead of the road.

"No, it's just that I'd like to see a bit of the Island."

"Mm, yes, right. If you say so. You'll need to keep your eyes open, though."

After another couple of minutes, Theo stopped the car in a narrow layby.

"There it is," he said, "over there."

"Where?"

"That big one."

An imposing grey stone house stood high above Bonchurch, sheltered at the back by the Downs and with a clear view out over the Channel to the south.

"Oh, Theo, it's lovely. Can you stop here for a moment so I can take a photo for my sister?"

"OK. I rang this morning before I came to fetch you, and they said we could have a look round. Can I go now?"

"Yes please. But not so fast."

When they reached the house, Theo drove slowly up the gravelled driveway and parked his Mini in the cobbled courtyard at the back of the hotel alongside the Volvo estates, Audis and Jaguars. They walked round to the front entrance.

"Oh, look," said Jenny, "there's the veranda where the photo was taken so this must be the house."

"Yes, looks like it. Do you want to go inside?"

"A quick look, yes, although it won't stir any memories for me. I'd much rather have a look round the outside and take some more photos."

For the best part of an hour, Jenny and Theo wandered around the immaculate grounds until a sudden squally shower sent them running for cover to a summerhouse beside the lawn.

"I can't imagine Great Aunt Mary and Grandma living here," said Jenny as she moved aside a sun lounger so she could see out of the window. "It should have been a lovely place to grow up, but I know Grammy didn't have a happy childhood. She and... she and... "

"She and who?"

"Oh, Theo – I've just seen something."

"What?"

"That big cedar tree over there, with the sloping lawn and the sea in the background, I've got a painting of it."

"How do you know that's it?" said Theo, coming to stand beside her.

"Because my aunt painted it. It's hanging in my sitting room. I see it every day."

The sudden and immediate connection to her great aunt, together with the close proximity of Theo, made Jenny's heart race.

"Oh, look," she said, "it's nearly stopped raining, I must take a photo for Sue. Be back in a moment."

Out in the open, Jenny was able to breathe more easily and she busied herself taking pictures from various angles. When she looked back at the summerhouse, Theo was framed in the doorway.

"Hold it there for a moment," she called, and took a couple of quick photos.

"You're getting wet."

"Not very," she replied. "Shall we go now?"

Theo dropped her off at the hotel. As she went towards the lift, one of the receptionists called her over.

"Mrs Holmes?"

"Yes."
"There's someone to see you. He's in the lounge."

Chapter 17

"Ben! What are you doing here? There's nothing wrong, is there?"

"Stop worrying, Mum, everything's fine."

"I swear you're taller than ever," she said as she hugged him. "How's Brighton going?"

"Fine, Mum, everything's fine."

"Well, why are you here? It's lovely to see you but why've you come?"

"Meggie rang me and gave me an earful for not ringing you, so I rang home and you weren't there and Dad didn't know where you were. He sounded a bit odd. I tried your mobile but you didn't answer, so I tried Auntie Sue. She only told me where you were if I didn't tell Dad. What's going on, Mum?"

"Your father and I had a bit of an argument and I needed some time away so I came to see Sue. Did she tell you why I'm in the Isle of Wight?"

"She was just off to see some Connie woman. She said it was something about a book."

"Let's go for a walk along the beach and I'll tell you all about it. You look a bit pale – are you eating properly?"

"Nothing but chips and fizzy drinks, dearest Mother. Come on, let's get out of here."

After walking one way along the shore line then the other, they settled down on the dry sand at the top of the beach with their backs against the sea wall.

"Why didn't she marry the poet?" asked Ben, as he knocked down the topmost pebble of their cairn with a well-aimed shot.

"I don't know. There's somebody helping me – he's gone to Newport Records Office this afternoon to see what he can find out about this Albert person, so he'll probably call me this evening."

"Maybe she got pregnant and he buggered off."

"Possible, but nice girls didn't sleep with their boyfriends in those days. That would have caused a huge scandal. Anyway, I reckon she'd have just had the baby and be damned to her family. She loved children. She was much kinder than your great grandmother. She was lovely. And sparkier. She was a ban-the-bomber, you know."

"Good on her. Listen, Mum, I've got things going on tonight so I'd best be getting back."

"Thanks for coming, darling, it was lovely to see you. Shall I drive you over to Ryde? Or Shanklin for the train?"

"Ryde would be good."

"OK. Ben?"

"Yes?"

"Don't tell your Dad where I am – I need a few more days on my own."

"Is it serious, Mum? This thing with Dad?"

"I don't know."

"You need to keep your phone on."

"And you need to ring me once in a while. Give me a haul up."

"Give us your hand, then. Soon be time for that wheelchair."

"Don't be cheeky," she said, as she brushed the sand from her clothes. "My car's behind the hotel. Do you want some lunch before you go?"

"It's alright, I'll get something in Southampton."

"Yes, probably chips and a burger. I'll get you some salad and a couple of sandwiches. The usual?"

"Yeah. Thanks."

Chapter 18

The drive to Ryde took longer than Jenny expected so she gave up on her plan to look round Bembridge on the way back in case Theo was waiting for her at the hotel. She concentrated on the road and tried not to think about whether she wanted to see him more than she wanted to find out about Albert.

His Mini wasn't outside the hotel and there weren't any messages for her at reception, so she collected her keys and went up to her room. She remembered Ben saying that Sue was going to see Connie so she rang her sister to see what had happened.

"No, she's not back, yet," said Duncan. "Went off in a bit of a hurry. Something about Connie."

"Connie's not ill, is she?"

"No, I don't think it was anything like that. I expect she'll call you as soon as she gets in."

"OK. How's the dog?"

"Doing well. How are you?"

"Doing well. Bye, Duncan."

Jenny didn't want to sit around in her room and wait for Sue to call or Theo to arrive, so she went into Ventnor to buy herself a sketch pad and some soft pencils; there was an image in her head which she needed to get down onto paper. She took her purchases back to the hotel and settled down in front of the picture windows overlooking the sea.

Intent on her work, she neither saw Theo's car pull up nor heard his voice until he sat down beside her.

"Hello, Jenny. I've got some news for you."

"Oh, how exciting." She shut her sketchbook and smiled at him. "That was quick."

"Mm."

"What is it, what's the matter?"

"Shall we go somewhere else? It's a bit public here."

"The beach?"

"No, tide's in. Let's go to the top of Boniface Downs. Come on."

They didn't talk much as Theo drove through Ventnor, up Down Lane and parked at the top of Boniface.

"Good view, isn't it," said Theo, as he parked the Mini and wound down his window. "Do you want to get out and have a look around?"

"No, I want to hear your news first."

"OK."

"What have you found out, Theo? Don't keep me in suspense. Is it bad?"

"Well, there's still a few loose ends to tie up, but I think I've got the basics right. I was searching in the records for any mention of your great aunt's name or the De Versey name and I found this."

He reached round the back of Jenny's seat and pulled forward a sheaf of papers.

"Here you are. This one first. Woodford must have been your great-great uncle's surname. It's from June 1920, the Isle of Wight Courier.

Local Families in Court Battle

Last Friday, a case of some interest was heard at Newport County Court when Mr. And Mrs. Reginald Woodford of Boniface House, Bonchurch, sought to re-establish a long-disputed boundary between their property and that of the adjoining property, Durcombe Grange, owned by Sir George and Lady de Versey.

Mr. S.M. Flux, representing the plaintiffs, argued that a lack of maintenance on the boundary wall by Lord

George and Lady de Versey occasioned debris to fall on land belonging to his clients, thus depriving them of its use. In addition, the line of the original boundary wall was now being used as a public footpath denying Mr. and Mrs. Reginald Woodford their right to privacy. Mr. Flux presented to the court Title Deeds, documents and maps in support of the plaintiffs' claim. The court found in favour of Mr. and Mrs. Woodford and ordered the litigants to restore a boundary wall, to be of not less than five feet, to its rightful place. In view of the fact that the litigants had been given every opportunity to settle the matter out of court, costs were awarded against them.

"Interesting. Did we see the wall this morning?" she asked.

"Must have done."

"Well, it shows that there was a bit of a feud going on between the two families, but it wasn't too bad. Why the long face?"

"Here's the next one. November the same year. Isle of Wight Courier again."

Gruesome Discovery

A lifeless body was pulled from the sea off Monks Bay Tuesday last. It is thought that the body had been in the sea for at least a week. Formal identification has yet to take place but the corpse is believed to be that of Mr. Albert de Versey, the twenty-one-year-old nephew of Lord George and Lady de Versey of Durcombe Grange. Lord George and his family are at present in Italy.

"Oh, no! Oh, my God, poor man. Whatever happened? And poor Grammy! Are you sure it's him? Maybe it was someone else."

"I'm afraid it was him – I checked the death register. Here's a copy."

Theo slid another sheet of paper onto her lap.

"It says there, look. Cause of death was given as drowning."

"Where?"

Theo took her hand and guided her fingers to the correct column.

"How terrible. No wonder Grammy didn't talk about him, it must have been too painful for her."

"Yes, must have been. But now we come to a problem. I was going to take you to see his grave but I can't find any record of his burial at St. Catherine's in Ventnor or at Boniface Parish Church. There are plenty of de Verseys in both churches, but no Walter. Now, why wouldn't he be there?"

"Because he was only a nephew? Maybe he was buried where he grew up. His mother must have wanted that."

"No, she died before him, I checked. Her husband was a de Versey but he died before the first world war. And Albert had no siblings. So, a bit of a mystery. But at least we know that he was living right next to your great aunt in Bonchurch so the likelihood is that they did know each other."

"That means the poem in the book really was written specially for her. Oh, poor Grammy. It was a beautiful poem. They must have truly loved each other. I think he must be buried somewhere else on the Island."

Theo was silent for a while.

"Do you know what I think?"

He twisted in his seat and took hold of both her hands.

"Whatever is it, Theo?"

"I think he committed suicide."

"Oh, no! How terrible. Why ever would he do that? And leave Great Aunt Mary? He wouldn't have done that, he loved her! You can tell by the poem. He wouldn't have done that, it's not possible. There must be another explanation."

"I found this, as well. I'm sorry. October the same year."

Jenny scanned through the wedding report of Agnes Bennett, niece of Mr. and Mrs. Woodford.

"My grandmother. It's interesting, yes, but what is there to be sorry about?"

"Read it carefully." He put his arm around her shoulders and waited for her to realise the implication of what she was reading.

"Oh, no! Why wasn't Grammy there? It's just before Albert died. Where was she? Why wasn't she there?"

Jenny burst into tears. Theo pushed a packet of tissues towards her then waited until she was calm again before he spoke.

"I don't know where she was but she certainly wasn't at the wedding. Are you sure you don't want to get out and have look round? Bit of fresh air might help?"

"Oh, I'm so sorry and you've been so kind. I'm so sorry, I really am, it's just that it's been a bad few weeks and I got a bit overcome and… and… "

"It's OK. It's fine, don't worry." He put his arm around her shoulders.

"Will you take me back to the hotel, Theo? I feel a bit of a wreck and I need to think about all this. I still can't believe it."

"Yes, probably not what you were expecting. I've got another idea about where Albert might have been buried, but I need to check it out with Grandad tonight."

"How is he?"

"Home from hospital tomorrow, I hope. I'll come to the Clifton tomorrow morning. You sure you'll be OK tonight?"

"Yes, I'll be fine. Can I keep these copies? I want to show them to my sister."

"Yes, they're for you."

She leant over and kissed him quickly.

"Thank you, Theo."

Once back in her room, Jenny went straight to the phone to ring her sister, but Duncan said that she was taking an evening surgery.

"Oh, sorry, I forgot what day it was. Tell her I'll be back tomorrow so I'll see her then. No need for her to ring me tonight, I'm for an early bed."

"What time tomorrow?"

"I don't know, I need to book a ferry. I'll ring when I know. Bye."

"Jen? You still there?"

"Yes."

"Listen, I know there's a bit of trouble between you and Geoff, but he was here yesterday. He's desperate to talk to you."

"Geoff came down to yours?"

"Yes. He's a bit cut up, Jen. Arrived on the doorstep last night. Sue wouldn't tell him where you were. She said you'd talk to him when you were ready."

"Is he still there?"

"Not with us, no."

"Oh, Duncan! I'm in a bit of a mess."

"A stiff G&T and something to eat is what you need."

"Yes, I think you're right. Bye, and thanks."

While she waited for room service to arrive, Jenny re-read all the information Theo had found. If the wedding report was accurate, she realised that perhaps her great aunt had deserted Albert.

When she eventually fell asleep that night, she had nightmares of Geoff and her great aunt changing backwards and forwards into different people and chasing her off cliffs, waking with a jolt and a pounding heart as she hit the rocks below.

The next morning she packed her bag, booked a ferry, settled her bill, then sat down in the lounge with a cup of coffee to wait for Theo.

Chapter 19

It was nearly lunchtime before Jenny saw the now familiar red Mini pull up outside the hotel and Theo leap out and come up the steps two at a time.

"Sorry, couldn't get away before," he said as he sat down beside her. "I had to wait for Grandad to get signed out and it took ages. How are you? I was worried about you."

"Well, it was a bit much to take in and I've had to do a lot of thinking about my Great Aunt. I still don't understand what happened."

"Maybe you never will."

"Maybe not."

"D'you think it will help to see Albert's grave? Grandad thinks he might be buried at the old church. They built a bigger one in the 1880s and now they only use the old one for carol services and the odd christening or summer evensong, that sort of thing, but Albert might have been buried there. Sometimes a vicar would refuse burial in consecrated ground if there was any rumour of suicide, but at the old church they might have been a bit more open-minded. Shall we go and look?"

"Yes, OK. Do you want coffee or anything first?"

"No, let's go and see what we can find."

Old St. Boniface Church was down a narrow lane and set behind a low stone wall. There was a lychgate and a winding flagged path leading up to the entrance.

"Well, it's certainly small," said Jenny as they got out of the car. "No wonder they had to build a bigger one. Oh, I wonder if he's here. It's very peaceful."

They stood quietly side by side for a moment enjoying the

calm surroundings, the silence broken only by a blackbird rustling around in the fallen leaves beside the gravestones and a distant murmur from the sea beyond.

"Yes," said Theo. "Very peaceful. Shall we start looking? You sure you want to do this?" he added when he saw that Jenny wasn't moving.

"Yes, sorry. Just thinking."

"Let's go round together."

They did a complete circuit of the church, examining every tilted and moss-covered gravestone, but found nothing,

"It could have been one of those ones we couldn't read," said Jenny. "Some of them are really old."

"Shall we go round once more?"

"No, I don't think it would do any good. Let's go back to the car. I've got to get back – I've booked a ferry for this afternoon."

"Hold on a minute, there's a few more over there, look, right up beside the hedge. I don't think we checked them."

Jenny watched as Theo made his way to the side of the churchyard. She saw him suddenly bend down and start to brush away debris from a gravestone set horizontally into the ground.

"Jenny! I've found him, he's here, come and look."

Albert de Versey
Poet and Writer
Born 1898 Died 1920
Forever in my Heart
MFB

"But if she really loved him and he was 'Forever in her Heart'," Jenny burst out, "Why on earth did she desert him just when he needed her? Where was she? On holiday? He might not have drowned himself if she was here. Why didn't she stay here with him?"

"I don't know, Jenny."

"Oh, I thought I would be upset to find his grave, but I'm not, I'm really angry. You can't say you love someone and then disappear just when they need you. Oh, poor Albert."

"If you think about it," said Theo, "she must have come back to commission the headstone. Nobody else did that, it must have been her."

"I can't think about anything at all at the moment, I'm all muddled up. Oh, let's go, Theo, I need to catch my ferry."

"What time did you say it was?"

"Four thirty."

"Let's go then."

"I'll just take a photo for Sue."

When they arrived in Ventnor, Theo got out of the car quickly and came round to open the passenger door for Jenny.

Instead of going straight into the hotel, they turned towards the sea and leant against the Promenade railings.

"Give my best – "

"It's been a – "

They both laughed.

"You first," said Theo.

"I was going to say give my best wishes to your grandfather."

"And I was going to say that I've enjoyed being with you."

"Oh, thank you for helping me, Theo. I couldn't have done it without you. Oh, no, I'm going to cry again."

"You've used up all my tissues. Come here."

He brushed a tear from her cheek with his thumb then put his arms around her waist and drew her towards him. She rested her head against his shoulder.

"You're an amazing woman, Jen and I don't want to say goodbye."

She put her hands around his neck and looked up into his face.

"Oh. Oh, Theo!"

They kissed for a long time and then hugged, rocking back and forth on the pavement, neither wanting to let the other go. Shouts from behind made them break apart.

"Stop him, stop him! Stop, Ricky, stop!"

A small child was racing towards them oblivious to his frantic mother chasing after him pushing an empty buggy.

Theo put out an arm and scooped up the runaway.

"And where are you going to in such a hurry?"

"Ice cream. I want an ice cream." He tried to wriggle down.

"No, you stay here for a minute, you need to wait for your mother. I expect she's got the money. What flavour are you going to have?" he asked as the child's mouth opened wide ready for a full-throated howl. "My favourite's sausage. Mmm, sausage ice cream is yummy."

Watching Theo's easy manner with the child, an image rushed into her head of Theo in a few years' time with a young wife and children of his own. She knew then that it was time for her to leave. He needed to go his way and she hers. As the mother caught up with her child and began to thank Theo, Jenny turned away. On the steps of the Clifton she looked back, waved and blew him a kiss.

Chapter 20

Once she had checked out of the hotel, the drive from Ventnor towards the ferry at Yarmouth should have only taken three quarters of an hour, but Jenny's thoughts went round and round in circles thinking about Geoff, Theo and her Great Aunt Mary. Tears streamed down her face and she had to stop the car on the Military Road above Brook Bay to blow her nose. When she realised she was using one of Theo's tissues another outburst of crying delayed her even further.

It was early evening before Jenny reached Buckthorn House. Sue and Duncan were both busy in the kitchen.

"Ah, there you are," said Sue, taking Jenny by both hands, kissing her and drawing her into the kitchen. "Do you want tea or something stronger?"

"I need tea, I've got a terrible headache."

"I'll put the kettle on. Oh, Jen, have you been crying? You look worse than ever."

"Well, thank you very much! I know I look a wreck but it's always so helpful when your nearest and dearest remind you. Where's the dog? Is she OK?"

"She's fine, she's out in the garden with Zip and Fly."

Jenny went to the window to look for Flora.

"She's having great fun out there, chasing around."

"Yes, she's getting on well. You can tell us what's been happening while we eat. Is it ready yet, Duncan?"

"Another quarter of an hour should do it, so you've got time for a cup of tea first. Go and sit down in the other room and I'll bring it in."

"Thanks, Duncan," said Jenny, blowing her brother-in-law a kiss.

All through the meal, Jenny talked about what had been happening on the Isle of Wight. She told Sue and Duncan about finding the house and Albert's grave and she showed them the newspaper reports that Theo had found.

"Oh, Sue, I just don't understand why Grammy wasn't at her sister's wedding. Albert died only a month later so I think she must have gone off on holiday and left him. Look," she held up the newspaper report, "it says the bride's sister was out of the country. He wouldn't have committed suicide if she was there with him. His grave was so sad. It said *Forever in my Heart* with Grammy's initials but he couldn't have been forever in her heart if she wasn't there."

"Did she put up the gravestone?" asked Duncan.

"I suppose so," said Jenny. "She must have had second thoughts about what she'd done and put it up to salve her conscience."

"Have you still got the book, Jen?" asked Sue. "The one with the poem in it?"

"Yes, but I won't keep it. There's no point anymore."

There was silence for a while as Sue and Duncan watched Jenny's face begin to crumple and her tears start to fall.

"I think that's enough for one night, don't you, Duncan? We know a bit more of the story, Jen, but we'll tell you tomorrow morning, not tonight."

"What more?"

"Tomorrow, Jen, tomorrow. You need a rest. But I'll just tell you one thing – Grammy did truly love Albert. Now, Duncan and I'll clear up in here, why don't you take Flora for a quick walk down to the river and back? It's still light enough. Come on, up you get," she added as Jenny made no effort to move. "I'll get Flora's lead. Come on, up you get."

"Yes, ma'am."

Chapter 21

By the time Jenny came downstairs the next morning, Sue was reading the paper at the kitchen table but Duncan wasn't there.

"An emergency," Sue explained, "trouble with a calving. He'll be back later. Do you want some toast and coffee?"

"Mm, yes please."

"You look much better."

"Thank goodness. If I'd got much worse I'd have started to frighten the horses. You don't mind what I look like though, do you Flora." She bent down to stroke the dog's head.

"While I make some more coffee, you go and get your camera so you can show me the photos. You did take some, didn't you? On that fancy camera Geoff gave you?"

"Yes, I've got some photos. Will you tell me all you know? About Grammy and Albert?"

"Yes, but photos first. And eat your toast."

"Would that be before I fetch my camera or after?"

"Let's leave the photos till last, Sue," said Jenny when she'd eaten her breakfast and they were sitting side by side on the sofa in the sitting room. "I'm desperate to know what you found out from Connie. It was Connie who told you what happened, wasn't it?"

"Yes, poor woman. I think she was glad to be able to tell someone at last. She talked for ages. I was going to take you over to see her, but I think you'd best hear it from me."

"Oh, my God, that sounds serious. Whatever happened, Sue?"

"Are you ready for this?"

"Hope so. It's not too bad, is it?"

"Yes, I'm afraid so." She reached out to hold her sister's hand. "The reason Grammy wasn't at the wedding was because she was in Baden Baden, expecting a baby."

"A baby? Grammy was expecting a baby?"

"Yes. And it was still-born."

"Oh, no! She had a baby and it was still-born? How dreadful. How do you know it was still-born? Maybe it was adopted or something?"

"Grammy would have never let her baby be adopted. And Connie saw the death certificate. A little girl. Called Alice Louise."

"That's both our middle names."

"Yes, I know."

"Do you think Mum knew?"

"She must have done,"

"Was it Albert's baby?"

"Yes."

"Did he know she was expecting his baby?"

"Connie wasn't sure. She said her father, our Great Uncle Edwin, was horrified when he realised the price his sister had paid for his articles and Agnes's wedding. He never wanted to talk about it and so Connie couldn't ask too many questions."

"Why did she go to Baden Baden to have the baby? She might still have lost the baby but at least she'd have had Albert. Oh, poor Grammy! All alone in Germany with no-one to support her."

"Great Great Aunt Sybil made her go."

"Oh no, it gets worse and worse."

"Apparently, when she found out that Grammy was having an affair with Albert, she made Grammy choose between Agnes's marriage and Edwin's articles or Albert. The social scandal of a sister having an affair in those days would have ruined Agnes's chances of marriage and Edwin was financially dependent on Sybil so she could call all the shots."

"Why on earth didn't she choose Albert?"

"I don't know. Maybe she didn't know she was pregnant at the time and thought she could write and tell Albert not to worry – that she'd be back soon. When he never replied she must have realised her letters weren't getting through so she wrote to Edwin and asked him to deliver a letter. He went over as soon as he could but it was too late."

"He was already dead?"

"Yes. Albert must've thought Grammy had deserted him. Connie said her father never forgave himself for not getting the letter there sooner. It was Edwin who bought her that little house in Oxford when she came back from Germany."

"Didn't she used to teach German Literature at the University?"

"Yes. She didn't come back to England until just before the Second World War so she must have been pretty fluent by then. Do you remember how she and Mum used to talk together in German at Christmas time?"

Jenny laughed. "Yes – Grandma used to get furious. There's no getting away from it you know, our Great Great Aunt Sybil was a world class bitch and a bully. How could she have been so mean? Sending Grammy away like that."

"And she cut Grammy out of her will. Edwin and our grandmother had a bit but the rest went to Leonard."

"Leonard? Who's he?"

"He was Sybil and Reginald's son, Mum's second cousin. He was a lot older than her and he lived up in London. I think he was gay."

"I wonder what Sybil thought of that. I suppose all this explains why Grandma and Grammy were never the best of friends. And I'm so glad that Grammy did keep Albert forever in her heart like it said on his gravestone. I was beginning to think she deserted him. Oh, Sue, it must have been awful for her, losing Albert and her baby. Geoff and I've got problems but nothing like that. And I've got a wonderful sister which Grammy never had."

"Can I have that bit in writing? About being a wonderful sister?"

"No way."

"Let's have another cup of coffee before the photos. Do you want a bit of brandy in yours?"

"Mm, yes please, I feel distinctly wobbly. Shall we take the dogs out and leave the photos till later? I need a bit of time to think about things."

"OK. We could go right along the river and treat ourselves to lunch at the King's Head. It's dog-friendly."

"Sounds good."

Chapter 22

It wasn't until early evening that Sue and Jenny sat down together to look at the photos. Zip and Fly were in the kitchen with Duncan, waiting for their tea, but Flora was sitting on Jenny's feet, resting her head against her knees.

"Who's that?" Sue asked when they came to the photo of Theo framed in the summerhouse doorway.

"It's Theo. He's the one who's been helping me."

"I thought it was going to be an old man with a smoker's cough."

"No, I told you on the phone – it's his grandson. The grandfather was in hospital."

"He's got a lovely smile."

"Oh, Sue, he was lovely all over. I'd have stayed with him forever given half a chance."

"Jennifer Louise, you're blushing! Did you fall for him?"

"Yes, totally."

"What did he think of you?"

"I think I can safely say our feelings were mutual. But he was so young!"

"How young?"

"Mid-twenties I think."

"That's not so terrible these days."

"Yes, but I was so muddled up about him and Geoff and Grammy I couldn't think straight. I walked away, Sue. Waved him goodbye."

"Are you going to get in touch with him?"

"No, I think I need to get over him. I've got to go home and sort things out with Geoff, but knowing how I felt about Theo, he might have felt the same about Brigitte. Oh, Sue, Theo was so kind and handsome and I think he really liked me."

"Well, I'm not surprised - you're very likeable, you silly woman."

"I don't think Geoff likes me much."

"Well, he looked pretty shattered when he came down here looking for you. I thought he was going to take after you and cry all over me."

"Is he still in Lymington?"

"Not sure. Why don't you give him a ring?"

"I don't know what to say."

"Stand up for yourself. Say what you want to happen. You're much freer than poor Grammy ever was in the 1920s. You've got the choice of what happens, not like her, getting sent off to Baden Baden. Stand up for yourself, Jen."

"I wish it was that easy."

"Make a start. You could forget about evening art classes to begin with and go and finish your art degree. Don't you remember Grammy saying that she wished she could have gone to art school but that Sybil wouldn't let her go?"

"That bitch again."

"You could go to Norwich School of Design and chalk one up on Sybil."

"Mm, yes, that'd be good."

"Are you going to ring Geoff?"

"I suppose I'd better."

"Here's the phone, then."

Sue tossed the phone onto the sofa and went out to the kitchen. Jenny sat with the phone on her lap, listening to the occasional rattle of crockery as the dishwasher was loaded. She heard the order to "Sit!" and then the dogs' biscuits being poured into their bowls. Flora shot out to the kitchen but was soon back again to sit beside Jenny.

Jenny dialled Geoff's number, put the phone to her ear, listened to the first couple of rings then cancelled the call. She went out to the kitchen.

"I can't talk to him on the phone, Sue, not tonight, I need to see him. Can you ring him and tell him I'll be home tomorrow?"

"Why don't you stay an extra day – we could have a morning at that spa place I told you about and relax for a while."

"No, I think I'd best get home."

"You want me to ring him then?"

"Please."

"Give us the phone. Shall I ring his mobile number?"

"Try home first."

Jenny watched as Sue dialled the number and then put the phone to her ear. They stood in silence as they waited for Geoff to answer.

"Aah, hello Geoff, it's Sue. Yes, I know. Jen will be home tomorrow... yes, tomorrow... yes, she's fine. Bit tired, but fine... no, she doesn't want to talk... yes, I'll tell her. Yes, I'm sure you are. Bye."

"How did he sound?"

"Very relieved. I've got a feeling he thought you wouldn't be back at all. Do you want to go back, Jen?"

Jenny smiled at her sister and brother-in-law who were both watching her intently.

"I'd rather stay here a bit longer, but Geoff and I need to talk. I don't know what's going to happen between us – maybe a trial separation for a while. I don't know. And I need to think about Megan and Ben as well."

"They'll be fine – you need to put yourself first for a while," said Sue.

"Yes, I will. I promise."

"And do your Art degree?"

"Yes, ma'am."

That night, for the first time in several weeks, Jenny slept soundly, stirring only once in the small hours when her bedroom door was nudged open and Flora jumped onto the bed and nestled down beside her.

"Oh, Flora," she said as she put her arm around the dog, "I'm sure you shouldn't be up here but you can stay, just this once."

Chapter 23

"Have you got everything, Jen?" Duncan asked as he put her bag on the back seat of her car.

"Yes, I think that's it."

"Have you got the old book?" asked Sue. "The one with the poem in it?"

"Yes, of course."

"And you're sure about taking Flora?"

"Yes, absolutely. Jump in, girlie."

"Here's her food, then," said Duncan. "Don't let her get too fat."

"What's Geoff going to say when you turn up with a dog?" Sue asked as she gave Jenny the lead.

"No idea. Maybe it'll be a nice surprise." She laughed, then hugged Duncan and kissed her sister. "Oh, I wish Grammy had had as good a sister as I've got. Thanks, Sue."

"No, don't start crying again, this dress is clean on. Drive carefully and don't forget to stop for a rest."

"OK, bossy-boots!"

"And this is for you tonight so you don't have to cook. It's a vegetable lasagne."

"Well, that's at least one thing sorted."

"Work on the rest, Jen, and don't forget to stand up for yourself."

"I'll try. See you both soon. Bye!"

When Jenny reached home that evening, Geoff hurried out to meet her.

"Who's this, then?" he asked when he opened the car door for her and Flora leapt out across Jenny's lap.

"It's Flora. She's a collie cross. Be gentle with her, Geoff, she's still a bit nervous around people."

"Oh, Jen! I'm so glad you've come home. Are you OK? Good journey? I rang Sue to see what time you'd left so I could get something nice for you to eat tonight. I got you a lasagne – you do like lasagne, don't you?"

"Yes, I still like lasagne."

"What's the dog's name again?"

"Flora."

"Who does she belong to?"

"Me, Geoff. She's my dog. Her food and my overnight bag are in the back, you take those, I'll take Flora. Come on, Flora, in you come."

Walking past the kitchen to the sitting room, Jenny noted the carefully laid table, the flowers and the bottle of wine.

"Shut the front door, Geoff," she called, "I'm going to let Flora off."

Standing in the sitting room, Jenny pulled her shoulder bag round to the front. She took out her great aunt's book and held it in her hands for a few moments, then put it in the bookcase, next to A Shell Guide to the Isle of Wight by Pennethorne Hughes. If things went well between her and Geoff, she would tell him all about her Great Aunt Mary but, for now, it was enough to be at home. She sat down on the sofa and Flora leant against her legs.

Several weeks later, a registered parcel arrived for Jenny. Inside was a letter from her sister and a small box.

Dearest Jen,

After you'd gone, I had another look through Grammy's jewellery to see if I still had that owl brooch because I was going to give it to you, but I found something better. The clasp was worn right through, so I took it to a jeweller to be mended. Try not to cry when

you see the inscription on the back.
Love,
Sue.
XXX
P.S. How is Norwich going?
P.P.S. Is Flora behaving?

Jenny opened the box. Inside, on a bed of tissue paper, was a gold heart-shaped locket with a delicate chain. On the front were two entwined initials, A and M, surrounded by flowers. Inside, half-covered by a twist of auburn hair, there was a photograph of a solemn young man with a broad forehead. The inscription on the back was barely discernible. Jenny lifted it up to the light. It read *Forever in my Heart.*

Jenny didn't cry. She sat with the locket in her hand and thought about her Great Aunt Mary and all the difficulties she had overcome. She lifted her hair away from her neck, fastened the chain, swung the locket round to the front and then went to the mirror.

"You can do it," she said to her reflection. "Believe in yourself and you can do anything."

Printed in Great Britain
by Amazon